RICHARD DENNING was born in Ilk lives in Sutton Coldfield in the We works as a General Practitioner.

He is married and has two chi been fascinated by historical settings .. as horror and fantasy. Other than writing, his main interests are games of all types. He is the designer of a board game based on the Great Fire of London.

You can find out more about Richard and his work on his website: www.richarddenning.co.uk

# The CATACOMBS Of VANAHEIM

## RICHARD DENNING

First published in 2013 by Mercia Books
www.merciabooks.co.uk

Revised Edition 2015

Copyright © Richard Denning 2013
www.richarddenning.co.uk

Graphics © Gillian Pearce
www.hellionsart.com

Anglo Saxons Runes are Germanic Font 2 from:
www.fontspace.com/dan-smiths-fantasy-fonts/
anglosaxon-runes with permission from Dan Smith

ISBN  978-0-95681-034-2 (paperback)

British Library Cataloguing in Publication Data
A CIP catalogue record for this book is available from
the British Library

# THE CATACOMBS OF VANAHEIM

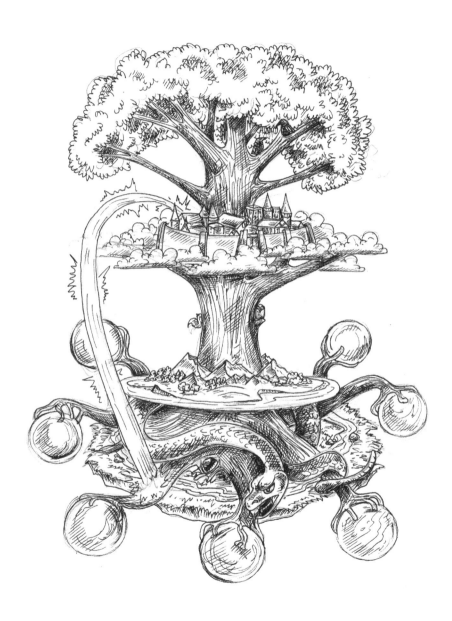

# Chapter One

## Training

"If you hold your shield like that, Anna, you will get killed in your first battle!" Meccus bellowed. "Hold it higher. You need to protect your belly, chest and neck – those are the vulnerable parts – but you keep dangling it down by your side." The blacksmith raised his own shield by way of demonstration, his muscular arms making light work of lifting the large circle of oak reinforced by iron studs and crowned with a central dome-like boss.

"But the thing is so heavy!" the red-haired girl complained, heaving the bulky wooden board up and then pulling it close to her chest.

"You were the one who wanted so much to be a shield maiden. What did you expect – that it would be easy?"

"No...but..."

"But nothing! Your father asked me to train you along with Lar and Wilburh and the older lads. I did not complain whatever I felt about the matter. However, I won't treat you any easier than the others – understand? If you want an easier life you can always leave the shield and go back to the kitchens and to sewing. Do you want that?"

He was rewarded with a flat expression. "Just tell me what to do," she replied.

Meccus shrugged, lifted his own shield and the wooden

practice sword and came towards her again. "That is better! With a sword it is hard to strike you anywhere mortal, protected as you are by the shield." He studied her for a moment. "Maybe you are right, however. The shield is perhaps a little large and heavy for you. I will give you a smaller one that will allow you to use your speed and agility better. You must be able to move about and get the best angle to attack your enemy. When you are fighting, swords, axe and spear are important, but don't forget that a shield can itself be a weapon. I'll show you."

He circled Anna and the girl watched him warily. Then he leapt forward and thrust the shield towards her face, the boss halting a mere inch from her nose. Anna gulped. Had Meccus not been so skilled the shield could have broken it; the mere thought made her eyes water.

He stepped back. "An attack like that can stun or incapacitate your foe and often will come from nowhere. It is important that you master the shield – it's the key to your defence. This is doubly so if Lar and Wilburh co-operate with you." He gestured that the two boys should join Anna.

Lar was sitting on a log nearby, eating an apple as he watched the training. With a groan, he tossed the apple core away, picked up a sword and another shield and came and stood by his sister. "Delighted to be here!" he said with a touch of gently taunting sarcasm and a wink at Anna.

Lar and Anna were the children of Nerian, the Headsman of their little village of Scenestane. Lar, who had almost no interest in martial skills, had to train as a warrior as all boys must, but he showed little talent for it and always, just as now, was reluctant to use a sword and shield. There was one discipline, however, in which he excelled. Lar was an exceptional shot with a bow. He was also a natural trader, good at negotiating with travelling merchants and tradesman who passed through the village. If Nerian wanted to strike a sharp deal on cloth or supplies, he always let Lar do the talking. The boy's youth usually unsettled the traders, and before they knew what had happened they were riding out of the village having left their goods behind, and their coin purse was rather lighter than they might have hoped.

While Lar was a reluctant warrior, his sister was not. Almost as soon as she could walk, she had begged their father to let her train like the boys did. At first he had refused, until

a few months ago when Anna and her friends had saved the village from the attentions of the evil sorceress, the fallen Valkyrie, Kendra, and her army of dark elves, the vicious Svartálfar. As a result, Nerian had relented. Now Anna was being tutored in the ways of the warrior, as were all the village youths.

"Come on, Wilburh, put down your sticks and get up here!" Meccus called again, his voice getting more irritated by the minute.

It was a fact that Anna was more enthusiastic about becoming a warrior than either Lar or Wilburh, who was more interested in ancient scripts and sorcery. Wilburh, a naturally brooding boy with fair hair and bright blue eyes, was studying under Iden, the village priest, his head full of strange words, old stories and at times frightening ideas. It left him little time for learning about spears and swords. Now Wilburh said nothing, but looked up from where he had been crouching, head low, staring down at some strange looking sticks, each the length of his palm. He scowled, thrust them into his pouch without comment and plodded over to stand on Anna's right.

"Finally! Now, overlap your shields," Meccus instructed.

Anna placed her shield so that it partially covered Lar's, while Wilburh covered Anna's on the other side.

"See how you protect each other like that?" As he spoke, Meccus stabbed and poked with the mock blade, but it only clattered against the wood and did not hurt them.

"Well done!" Their friend, Ellette, who was in fact Meccus's daughter, was nearby with Wilburh's twin sister, Hild. The two girls had come to watch the training and were clapping and shouting encouragement. Neither was skilled with a sword, but Ellette was a superb shot with a sling and was sorting through a handful of stones, selecting the most balanced ones from the pile in her lap. Maybe because she was so small she was also agile and could climb like a squirrel. Her small size and dextrous nature had earned her the nickname 'Little Elf'. At this very moment she was sitting on the bough of the tree she had clambered up a few moments before. Perching there, she examined the pebbles one by one, popping the best ones into the pouch at her belt and tossing the others to the ground, narrowly missing Hild.

In contrast with her twin brother, Hild was bright and bubbly in nature. She was, however, no climber and preferred to stay at ground level. At present she was investigating some plants that grew at the base of the tree in which her friend was nesting. Hild was learning all about herb lore and medicines from her mother and spent most of her time rooting around in the woodlands near their village of Scenestane, looking for herbs to use in her healing potions.

They were close to Scenestane right now. Meccus had brought them to the meadow near an ancient barrow. The grass-covered mound was a burial place of the 'Old People' – folk that had lived and died here centuries ago, a long forgotten people who had built the hill forts and stone circles that littered the landscape. Anna's people, the Angles of Mercia, were relative newcomers, having settled here less than 100 years before, long after the Old People had gone.

The entrance way of the tomb, which was engraved with runes and mystical arcane markings, was no ordinary door to a burial crypt. It was in fact an opening of the Bifrost, the rainbow bridge that connected Anna's own world of Midgard – otherwise called Earth – to all the other Nine Worlds of the Universe. Through it the Valkyrie sorceress, Kendra, had fled after her defeat in the summer, but not before she had broken the law of the gods and opened the portal so that free passage between all of the Nine Worlds was now possible.

Some of those worlds were home to ferocious monsters. So Nerian, fearing an attack or, even worse, an invasion had placed a watch on the doorway every day since Kendra had gone. Yet in the weeks since the Battle of Scenestane no one had arrived through it. The leaves in Ellette's tree were already turning gold, red and yellow. The summer heat had left them some days before, and the air was cooler and damp with the threat of autumnal showers. Now that summer was over without any visitors, friend or enemy, some in the village had suggested that this endless vigilance was a waste of time. Nevertheless, Nerian insisted that they continue their careful watch on the portal, and so Meccus had brought the children here today so they could take their turn at watching the Bifrost while they were training.

Perhaps because nothing had come through the portal all summer, after the briefest glance at the entrance when they had arrived, the children had stopped looking at it. Meccus was focussing on having them march back and forth in their small shield wall. Hild had wandered a short distance away and was busily placing various leaves into different little pouches for processing later. So it was Ellette, sharp-eyed and sharp-eared, who first heard a high-pitched sound coming from the doorway. Looking up, she noticed that the dull stone slab blocking the tomb was glowing and a myriad of colours was swirling and flashing across it.

"Er...look out! Someone is coming through the Bifrost!" she shouted, scrambling down from the branches. She was soon standing at the base of the tree, sling held in one hand and a dozen pebbles in the other.

They all turned towards the barrow and stared entranced at the flashing colours. Of them all, only Anna had travelled through the Bifrost. She had been accompanied by their friend and companion, the dwarf, Gurthrunn, whom they had met during the adventures that led to the battle with Kendra. On that occasion Gurthrunn had taken her to Asgard. There she had met the Goddess Freya, the God Heimdall and the greatest god of them all, Woden, the All Father, who in gratitude had given her a sword. It was a beautiful weapon and it now lay in its scabbard on the grass, along with everyone else's weapons, close to where they were practising.

Meccus was first to recover from his surprise. "Quick, everyone, get your weapons. Hild, call the alarm!"

Stirred into life, they rushed to the pile of weapons. Anna seized her sword. Lar, throwing down his wooden practice weapon, picked up his bow staff and quickly strung it from the bowstring he carried in the pouch at his belt. He then grabbed half-a-dozen arrows from his quiver and stuck them in a line in the ground. Wilburh reached for his own seax, but then changed his mind and instead fumbled inside the leather pouch at his waist. In a moment he had retrieved the bundle of sticks, each about the length of his hand and each carved with runic lines and angular letters that only he and his tutor, Iden, could understand.

In the fight against Kendra the children had discovered that Wilburh was able to use magic and sorcery, and he had proven far better at that than with any weapon. Wilburh had been ignoring the training and had in fact been studying the rune sticks given to him by Iden. The priest used them to help call upon the gods, asking them to bless and protect the village. Wilburh, though, had studied the sacred scrolls Iden kept in the temple, and in them had discovered words that could be used for sorcery: words to call upon the elements and control them. In a moment of crisis during that earlier adventure, Wilburh had found he could use the sticks to cast magical spells. He had created light and fire and even calmed a dangerous snake. Despite these marvels, he felt there was more for him to learn, and most days he would either lie around on the ground or sit at a table, a scroll unrolled nearby. Then, clutching the rune sticks he would recite combinations of words, trying to learn more spells; trying to master this new art. Now, as he readied his sticks, he considered which incantation to try.

Hild, who always carried a horn at her belt, put it to her lips and drew a deep breath. As she did so, the others exchanged a glance, each thinking back to another horn: one with which they were very familiar. Earlier in the summer, it was finding the horn belonging to the God Heimdall that had projected them all into adventure and brought about their fight with Kendra, who wanted it for herself. The horn, from which only Anna had been able to draw out a sound, was able to summon an army to fight at the command of its master or mistress. Alas, Anna had been obliged to return the golden horn to Heimdall. Hild's was merely an ordinary instrument fashioned from an ox-horn. It was, however, capable of producing a loud blast, and the echoing sound would carry to the village. As soon as the villagers heard the alarm call, they would arm themselves and rush to answer it.

The Bifrost was glowing brighter now. In fact it was almost too bright to look at. There was one last flash, and suddenly the rainbow was gone and instead a brilliant white light showed through the doorway. As their eyes adjusted, the children could see a field of snow through the portal. In the distance, immense mountains rose up, while just on the other side of the door was a flat plain. Shapes were moving across this plain towards them. They were indistinct at first, but as they approached the portal, they came into focus and the children saw that they were shaped like men: huge men, each with a head, two arms and two legs. But that was as close as their resemblance to humans came. Their skin seemed to be a silvery blue-white colour.

As he studied them, Wilburh could see that their skin was not like a man's, warm and pink and full of blood, but in fact looked like ice. It seemed incredible, but as the creatures approached their side of the Bifrost and he studied them more closely, he had no doubt that they were indeed made of ice. The being closest to the portal stepped through and stomped on the path that led from the barrow door. Wherever he trod, ice spread out from beneath his feet and froze the grass, and as the iceman advanced away from the portal, so too did the blanket of ice. It spread out from the door and clawed its frosty way forward across the meadow towards them.

Wilburh's gaze was drawn upwards, along powerful thighs, past a strong torso to an ice-white face. Silvery eyes fixed the children and blacksmith in their gaze. Slowly the being lifted its arm and pointed sharp, icicle-like claws at Hild.

"Look out!" Wilburh shouted as a storm of hailstones blasted out of the creature's palm towards his sister.

# Chapter Two

## Ice Elementals

Like lightning, Anna threw herself in front of Hild, bringing her shield up to protect them both. An instant later the hailstones clattered against it. One stone, missing the shield, sped on past the board and bounced off Hild's shoulder.

Dropping her horn, Hild screamed with the pain and clutched at the wound with one hand, blood oozing through her tunic and between her fingers.

"Keep calling!" Anna shouted.

Despite the pain, Hild nodded, scrambled on the grass for the horn, retrieved it, took a deep breath and sent forth another blast.

More of the ice beings stepped through the portal so that now there were six of them on the children's side of the Bifrost. They were spreading out, each heading towards a different opponent. Seeing one approaching her, Ellette spun the sling furiously before she released the stone, her arm a blur. The stone hurtled towards the enemy and smashed into its chest. In a shower of ice fragments, the iceman was knocked over onto its back.

"I got one!" Ellette shouted cheerfully, and then stared in disbelief as the creature climbed to its feet and stumbled on towards her.

"Never mind!" she said, backing away and loading another pebble into her sling.

Lar let fly with an arrow that caught one of the ice creatures in the torso, punching right through so that the arrowhead protruded on the far side of its chest. The creature's scream of pain was like the sound of an icy wind echoing along a mountain pass. Like Ellette, Lar was convinced he had killed the creature. He gawped as it reached behind, took hold of the arrow head, broke it off and, pulling the rest of the arrow out, snapped it in two and moved on towards Lar.

"Merciful Woden," Lar exclaimed as he notched another arrow on his bow, "they're indestructible!"

Anna moved closer to Meccus, and the two locked shields and advanced towards a group of three ice creatures that were closing in on them and Hild. The group now began to run at them.

"Stand firm, they are trying to knock us over!" the blacksmith shouted.

Anna braced herself, preparing for the charge.

Sure enough, the ice men's shoulders barged into the shields. Anna and Meccus staggered back a few steps, but the blacksmith's immense strength kept them on their feet. The three creatures roared at them and then punched and pounded at the shields with fists like sledgehammers. One of the three stepped away and waved its hands back and forth. The fists changed shape, flattening into icy blades with fearsome sharp edges. It advanced on them again, swinging its arms like great swords. One chipped a chunk of wood off the top of Anna's shield. She stabbed back and connected with the ice beast, the point of her sword plunging deep into its arm. Yet again there was that loud high-pitched screech of pain and outrage.

"Well done, Anna!" Meccus bellowed as he too hacked at his opponent.

Wilburh, shocked and muttering beneath his breath "They must be elementals!" became aware that one of the creatures was moving towards him, this one carrying a sharply pointed spear. The ice monster's arm went back in readiness to throw the weapon. Wilburh raised one hand and pointed it at the enemy. He focused on the rune sticks, drawing on their power as he spoke the words that should rain destruction on the advancing beast.

"*Heoruflá æledfýr!*" he shouted and then frowned when there was no response. The words meant '*fire arrow*'. They should have summoned a missile of fire and flung it at the ice creature. This is what had happened in the battle against Kendra. But today nothing happened – no fire, no arrow – nothing at all, in fact. Ten paces away the ice beast paused and studied him, its head tilted to one side as though curious about what Wilburh was doing. Then it once again strained in readiness to release the spear.

Panicking, Wilburh tried again, hastily repeating the words. Still no fire bolt. All that happened was a fairly feeble blast of warm air projected from his hand towards the ice beast at the precise moment that the creature released the spear. Although the spell had absolutely no effect on this creature, the blast of air was just strong enough to deflect the spear about an inch in its flight, changing its course so it whistled past, barely missing Wilburh's neck and hurtling away into the distance. He shook his head, baffled by the failure of his spell to have any effect on the ice creature.

The enemy smirked a humourless smile and advanced again, creating a blade of ice out of its hand just as the other had done and swinging it about, obviously intent on slicing Wilburh in two. Stumbling backwards, he tripped over his own feet and tumbled head over heels. As he struggled to get up off the ground, slipping and sliding on the spreading ice, he became aware that the creature was now standing right over him, glaring down with a terrifying expression in its eyes: an intense coldness, without any hint of compassion; a coldness that seemed entirely appropriate for a creature made of ice. In desperation, Wilburh raised one hand and tried to summon the mystical energies needed to create a shield out of the air between him and the terrifying beast.

"*Lyffc bordrand!*" he shouted, and there was a brief shimmering in the air above him. '*Air shield*', he had called, creating a mystical barrier out of the very air, which should have been strong enough to withstand any blow no matter how ferocious. However, when the ice man stabbed his blade-hand at it, the shield simply shattered as though made of fragile glass. The creature now pulled back his arm and swung his blade-hand forward again, this time aiming at Wilburh's neck.

Suddenly, before the blow could land, the creature's chest shattered and fragments of ice scattered in all directions. A huge steel hammer head burst out from the gaping hole it had created in the ice man's body and spun away over Wilburh's head, finally thumping into the ground just five feet away.

As Wilburh gawped, the beast looked down in horror at the huge chasm in its chest, gave a last shout of pain and outrage, fell to its knees and then toppled face forward onto the grass, quite dead. An instant later there was a blur of motion, and Wilburh saw Gurthrunn, the mighty Dweorgar warrior, hurtle past him, retrieve his hammer, and with a roar go charging off towards the next ice elemental.

Catching his breath, his mind still coming to terms with the sudden appearance of the warrior dwarf who had saved his life and who presumably had just arrived through the Bifrost, Wilburh dragged himself to his feet, picked up his rune sticks and looked about him. Lar and Ellette were still firing stones and arrows at their opponents, chipping off ice fragments with every hit, but it seemed these elemental creatures were very hard to kill. Now that Gurthrunn had joined them, however, knocking one foe backwards and facing off against another, his war hammer appeared to be doing far more damage.

Beyond Gurthrunn, Meccus and Anna remained standing in their shield wall, their enemies still hammering against the wooden shields. One ice elemental was clearly badly injured, but the other two were unhurt, and if anything seemed spurred on by a feeling of vengeance for the death of their companion, their attacks becoming even more ferocious.

Behind Anna, the injured Hild was still blowing her horn, calling desperately for help, but she was running out of puff and the sound was becoming weaker and weaker. She blew the alarm call one more time and at last it received a reply. It came from the clump of trees that grew south of the barrow; beyond the trees was a stream, and on its far bank lay Scenestane.

A moment later the tree line was filled by a dozen villagers, boys and men, all with shields, spears or swords. Nerian, leading them, barked out a command, and with a clattering of wood the villagers formed up into a shield wall. Spears were thrust forward over the tops of shields to form a deadly barrier of iron. Another barked order followed, and in formation the villagers marched out towards the beleaguered children.

The five remaining ice elementals snarled at the new arrivals and backed off to gather in a cluster. Soon enough the villagers reached the barrow, absorbing Anna and Meccus into their number so that the two battered defenders now stood in the centre of a shield wall of fifteen. They all began to move forward, pushing the elementals back towards the portal. Lar scampered around the edge of the shield wall and continued with his barrage of arrows. He hit one creature and it fell to the ground, and this time did not get up.

Gurthrunn bellowed a war cry and, running past the flank of the village shield wall, leapt into the middle of the other four elementals, his hammer smashing back and forth, shattering limbs and heads. The final pair of ice creatures flung volley after volley of large hail stones at the shield wall. Inevitably some found a mark and two of the villagers were struck on the head and knocked senseless, blood pouring from their wounds. Hild, one hand still clutching her injured shoulder, rushed to their aid, her other hand already reaching inside the pouches at her belt for healing herbs and dressings.

Meanwhile, Ellette had sneaked around behind the enemy and managed to smash a fair-sized sling-stone into the back of one ice creature's head. Already wounded, the beast fell dead to the ground. The final enemy warrior hesitated, turned and flung itself back through the Bifrost... and was gone. All that remained were clumps of ice that were beginning to melt, the ice water sinking into the grass of the barrow.

There was a moment's silence, and then, blowing their horns and cheering, the villagers celebrated their victory. Out of the shield wall Nerian emerged. He first rushed over to Anna and peered anxiously at her.

"Are you unhurt, Daughter?"

"I am fine, Father, don't fuss so," Anna replied.

"Anna, you are my daughter. I might have agreed that you can be a shield maiden, but that does not mean I am not going to worry about you!" he said with a worried frown. "Come here, girl."

She scowled as her father hugged her. Eventually she struggled free of his embrace. "I said I am fine," she snapped irritably.

"I am alright too, Father, thanks for asking!" Lar said,

looking hurt, but hiding it with gentle sarcasm.

Nerian just nodded at him. "Glad to hear it," he said shortly, turning away.

"Typical," Lar muttered, so softly that only Meccus heard. It was clear the boy was stung by his father's apparent lack of affection.

"Don't worry, lad," the blacksmith commented. "Nerian loves you too – he just finds it hard to show it. It's different with a daughter, lad. You're his son and will be Headsman one day. He does not want you to appear soft in front of the men."

Lar grunted a response, then seeing Anna's face flushed red with embarrassment as their father moved away, observed dryly, "By the look of things my sister is not happy either."

Meccus shrugged. "It will take Nerian time to adapt to Anna being a warrior, and she too must learn, not only how to be a warrior, but a woman and a daughter as well, all at the same time. It will not be easy for her."

They stood and watched Nerian walk across to the dwarf and shake Gurthrunn warmly by the hand. "That is twice you have helped us, Master Dweorgar," he boomed. "We owe you much."

"The friendship of your people is reward enough," Gurthrunn said, shaking his head. "In truth I arrived late on in the battle. You must give thanks to the blacksmith and the shield maiden and also her companions more than to me. To hold six of these elemental creatures at bay was no mean task."

"Indeed." Nerian smiled, turning to address the others. "Well done, you all did well. Doubly well done to you young ones, you fought like seasoned warriors. Come, we will return to my hall and open a barrel of mead to celebrate our..."

Gurthrunn interrupted him. "Headsman, we must talk," he said urgently.

Nerian grunted. "Then let us hear what you have to say over a drink."

"Very well." The Dweorgar nodded his agreement.

The villagers began returning to Scenestane, Nerian leading the way with Gurthrunn by his side. Soon, but for the fresh guard that Nerian had left to watch the Bifrost, everyone had gone from the barrow – except one. With curiosity in his gaze, the solitary guard studied the boy, clearly wondering why he had not gone with the others.

Wilburh sat alone on a small hump of grass near the barrow. In one hand he was still holding the rune sticks, his forehead deeply furrowed as he moved them around and stared at them. Eventually he put the sticks back into his belt pouch and buried his face in his hands.

The guard hesitated, unsure what he should do, for it was clear the boy was distressed. In the end he moved over to Wilburh.

"Is everything alright, lad? Why don't you go back to the village and join in the celebration?"

"It didn't work," said Wilburh, tilting his head to stare up at him. "I don't understand…what went wrong? It should have worked. Why didn't it work?"

The guard had no answer.

# Chapter Three

## Council

Eventually it started raining. Leaving the lone guard to take shelter under a nearby ash tree, Wilburh dragged himself to his feet and plodded back to the village, splashing carelessly through puddles. There he found that everyone had gone to the Headsman's hall. As he entered the hall, he saw the fire burning high in the fire pit, the villagers deep in animated conversations about the battle against the ice creatures. Still deep in gloom, he found the warmth, light and chatter did not comfort him.

His mother, Juliana, put down a jug of ale and rushed over to him. "Where have you been? I was worried about you."

"I was just...thinking," he mumbled.

Juliana looked into his face, nervously running her hand through her hair. "It strikes me that you spend rather too long thinking, Wilburh. It's not natural in a boy your age. I will talk to Iden. Maybe you should stop studying under him."

Wilburh glared at her. "No! Don't do that," he snapped.

"You're sure? If it's upsetting you, maybe you could go and study with Meccus instead."

"What, and learn to be a blacksmith?" Wilburh scowled. "Honestly, Mother, do you really see me working in a forge?"

She looked at her son's thin frame and far from muscular

arms. "Well...you are young yet. You still have time to fill out a bit," she said, but not very convincingly.

Wilburh shook his head. "No, Mother, I will always be weedy and you know it. Stop fussing, I will be fine. I just need...I just need food," he lied. He was not hungry at all, but it seemed to please his mother who rushed him over to the tables and went off to fill a platter with food for him.

When she had scurried away, Wilburh looked around the hall. The villagers were joining him at the tables now, eager for the jars of mead and trays of roast fowl that were being carried in. As they all sat down to eat, he saw Meccus leaning over to Gurthrunn. Wilburh edged closer, squeezing into a place next to Anna on the long bench.

"Merciful Woden, but what a fight," Meccus bellowed. "The youths did well," he added, looking at each of the children in turn. His gaze became uncertain as it lingered over Wilburh for a moment before moving on, as if he was unsure what to say to him. The blacksmith knew nothing of magic and sorcery, but must have been aware that all was not right with him. Wilburh caught Anna looking at him too. She seemed about to say something, but Nerian, who sat at the head of the table in the Headsman's chair, spoke first.

"What were they – those creatures of frost and ice?" he asked. "Master Dweorgar, can you tell us?"

Gurthrunn, who had just taken a huge bite of meat, tossed the partridge leg onto his plate, washed his mouthful down with a big gulp of mead, belched, and then wiped his mouth and beard with the back of his hand before answering.

"It is as I feared, and as the gods feared also. When Kendra opened the Bifrost, she opened up your world of Midgard to invasion from *any* of the Nine Worlds. The creatures that attacked your village today were elementals

– by which I mean spirits that have taken physical form. Elementals can in fact take many different forms, but these were created from ice. They come from the world of Niflheim – the coldest of the worlds. There all is covered in ice or frost." The Dweorgar paused to take another gulp of mead. "This was just a raiding party," he went on, "scouts sent to investigate how well Midgard is defended. Remember the surviving elemental – the one we allowed to escape? I am sure it will report back that you are not easy to defeat. I am hopeful that will buy you some time as they will be wary of attacking again, at least for now."

"But why would they want to?" Anna asked. "It's not like Midgard is always cold. Wouldn't they be uncomfortable in our summer?"

Gurthrunn shrugged. "Maybe, but elementals are strong and vengeful. Without a doubt they will be back one day. And they are only the first. There will be other creatures to threaten your village so long as the Bifrost remains open. We must do something about that," he said, taking another bite of roast fowl.

Nerian nodded thoughtfully. Meanwhile, Juliana had placed a plate overflowing with meat in front of Wilburh. She stood by him until he picked up a chicken wing and chewed on it. Then, looking happier, she went off to find her own seat. Once she had gone, he dropped the wing back on his plate, finding that he still had no appetite.

"The children fought well," said Nerian, raising his glass to Gurthrunn, "but I am grateful that you came when you did. Gods, but that hammer of yours is a fierce weapon. It is not Thunor's hammer by any chance, is it?" he added with a wink.

"Alas, it is not *Mjolner*, no. The hammer of the Thunder God is safe in Asgard. Kendra and her sisters did not steal that, thank the gods!"

Nerian and Gurthrunn emptied their mugs, and Nerian topped them both up again. "Well now," he said, "don't get me wrong, noble Dweorgar, your sudden arrival in the battle at the Bifrost was most welcome, but I sense you have a reason for returning to us. A reason to do with Kendra, perhaps – or the Bifrost – am I right?"

The Dweorgar nodded and took another swig of his mead before answering. "Well, it is true that my arrival was not a complete coincidence, yes."

"Oh, in what way?" Nerian asked.

"The ice creatures are not a loyal race. They are full of opportunists and traitors against their own kind. One such being sold me information that a raid upon Midgard was planned. As it so happened, Woden was about to send me on a task, but he permitted me to detour to warn you. I was a little late." He smiled. "I am actually on my way to Vanaheim, the world of the Vanir gods who are powerful in magic and wisdom. The reason I am going I cannot at this time tell you, but as it happens, the solution to your problems could lie in Vanaheim."

"How so?" Leaning back in his chair, Nerian supped at his mead and nodded for the dwarf to go on.

"Well, as I said, with the Bifrost open, anything with the wit to navigate the way can come through it, as you saw today. There are many creatures out there in the Nine Worlds that might threaten your village…and the ice elementals are not the worst of them, believe me."

"But we fought them off easily enough," Nerian boasted.

"You fought off six, with my aid."

"Even without you, I think we would have defeated them."

The dwarf nodded. "Yes, I believe you would. But that was a mere scouting party. Niflheim has millions of such creatures. Do you believe you could have handled a dozen, or 100...or 1,000?"

Nerian's face blanched at the thought. "A *thousand* of them? Is that possible?" He sat forward, his voice much less confident than before. Around the room there were shocked gasps at the very idea.

Gurthrunn laid a kindly hand on the Headsman's shoulder. "Believe me when I say that your race is not prepared for what horrors dwell among the Nine Worlds."

"You doubt our valour?" Nerian bristled.

"Never! I have seen you fight. But there are beings out there that make Kendra or those ice elementals seem tame. Creatures that terrify me, and even some that frighten the gods themselves."

Nerian's face grew even paler. "What do you suggest then?"

"I believe Vanaheim has the answer. The Vanir gods who live there can provide you with powerful magic to construct wards and defences strong enough to protect your village. Woden has suggested that you send ambassadors to make contact with the Vanir. I will make the introduction."

Leaning back again, Nerian considered the suggestion for a moment, then nodded. "It makes sense, but who shall we send on this task?"

Gurthrunn pointed at Anna. "The shield maiden is known to the gods. News of her name and deeds has reached Vanaheim. If she leads the company then the Vanir will grant her admission."

"No." Nerian shook his head. "That is too much of a risk. I will not send my daughter."

Anna stood up and glared at him. "Father, I am thirteen now, and you have accepted that I become a warrior. Would you not trust a warrior under your command? If so, why not your daughter?" she asked.

"Yes, I would, but you are still young, Anna."

"I am almost old enough to marry. In any event, young or old I was given my sword by Woden himself. I should be the one to go, and the others should go with me."

Nerian snorted. "Even if I accept for the moment that you do go, if you think I am going to send ten and eleven-year-olds like Ellette, Wilburh and Hild, you are mistaken. Even Lar is young at twelve. I will not risk them, nor will I risk the success of this enterprise by sending ones so young. There are older warriors we should send."

"Father, have you forgotten already?" Anna shouted, her face flushing with frustration. "If it had not been for those very ten and eleven-year-olds, not to mention Lar and me, this village would still be run by Kendra and you would not be here at all!"

From the other end of the hall, Ellette got to her feet and shouted, "We defeated her, and we did not run away when the ice creatures attacked either."

"Hush, child," Meccus chided his daughter. "I would not wish you to go. It is too dangerous."

"Then you will have to lock me up. Not that you should even bother, for you all know I would escape and go after Anna."

Meccus frowned, but he clearly knew she was speaking the truth. He turned to Gurthrunn. "Surely there are others who could go instead of Anna?" Nerian was nodding his agreement. The dwarf, however, shook his head.

"Nerian, Meccus," he said quietly, "I am content that Anna and her companions can be trusted to serve the village well. The gods have heard of Ellette, Wilburh, Hild and Lar. They have requested that they accompany Anna. Can you not accept their wisdom?"

"But what of the children's youth?"

"Age is not important to the gods, Headsman. They that have lived aeons do not think about age, they think only of character and ability. Your village youths were the first to oppose Kendra and were important in her defeat. For that the gods are happy to trust in them, and so should you be."

"There you go, Father," Anna said, one eyebrow raised in challenge. "If the gods will it, would you dare go against it?"

Seeking support, her father looked over at Iden. The priest glanced at Anna, then shrugged. "If it is truly the wishes of the gods then I will not speak against it, Nerian," he answered, but there was a tinge of doubt in his voice.

Nerian grimaced. He was not one to oppose the will of the gods any more than Iden was, yet he clearly was not happy about sending the children into danger. Deep furrows on his forehead betrayed a struggle between obedience to the Æsir – the gods of Asgard – and the feeling that he did not want to risk the young ones. "I am still not sure it is right…" he said at last, his voice trailing away as he glanced across at the twins' mother.

"It is most certainly *not* right!" Juliana said. She was on her feet at the far end of the hall, glaring across the room at Iden, Nerian and Gurthrunn. Her face was set with a determined expression that Wilburh and Hild knew only too well. "I am not risking my daughter and my son travelling to a strange world."

"But the Æsir have made their will clear," Gurthrunn argued, his face equally stubborn. "They must go!"

"Let the gods come here and tell me that for themselves then," Juliana shouted back, a flush of anger on her cheeks. The fact of her having spoken out now seemed to awaken second thoughts in Meccus.

"They *are* very young, Nerian," he said.

"Father!" Ellette objected.

Nerian thumped his seax hilt on the table, the sudden noise drawing everyone's attention. "Quiet, everyone! Let me think for a moment," he commanded.

In the sudden hush that followed, Nerian took a deep breath before speaking again. "Let us look at this in a different way. If I agree that Anna can go, then someone must travel with her to learn the sorcery. Who should it be? Which of us has the power to handle such magicks?" He looked across the table at the priest. "Iden, what about you? You are the obvious choice."

Iden shook his head. "I can read the runes, Headsman, but I have not the power to make them sing. Simple blessings and cantrips I can manage, but *real* sorcery? We all know that of those of us in the village there is only one who can do such things. Wilburh is the boy to send."

At the back of the hall, preoccupied and still playing with his food, which as yet he had barely touched, Wilburh had not really been listening to what was being said. He became suddenly aware of the silence, and looking up saw that everyone in the room was staring at him. His mother wore a worried frown and looked close to tears. Most of the villagers were studying him with curiosity in their gaze, but he was used to that – they all thought he was strange. Nerian and Gurthrunn both seemed to be appraising him as though expecting a response. Trying to recall their recent exchange, Wilburh gulped. Had they asked him a question? He didn't think so.

Clearing his throat, Nerian did now ask him a question. "Answer me honestly, boy. Can you really do this?"

Unsure what it was he was being asked to do, Wilburh stared blankly back at the Headsman, relieved when Nerian expanded on the question.

"If I allow you to go with Gurthrunn and Anna, boy, can you bring back these magicks? Can you handle them and can you control them?"

*What a time to ask a question like that*, Wilburh thought.

"Well, can you?" Nerian prompted when once again he didn't respond.

Wilburh shrugged. "I can try," he answered.

# Chapter Four

## Through the Bifrost

The following morning the children were up at dawn preparing for their journey. They were gathered in the hall again. Nerian and Juliana bustled around them making sure they had all that they might need for the journey.

"Did you remember to add mugwort to this broth, Hild? It will help counter any poison that has got into your wound. How does it feel this morning?"

Hild nodded as she held a crock pot up and her mother poured a sweet smelling green-coloured liquid into it from a pan she had just brought in from the kitchen.

"It's fine, just a scratch," Hild said, flexing her arm and moving her shoulder.

"Very well," Juliana went on as she placed the pan down on one of the long tables. "Now check your pouches. Do you have fennel, plantain, stune, cock's spur?"

"I have it all packed."

Juliana looked flustered. "What about chervil and...have you packed your pestle and mortar?"

"Mother, it's alright. I have everything I need in this." She held up her pack, which like her sling was made from thin leather. It was gathered at the top with a drawstring and had two woven fabric straps so it could be worn on her back, leaving her hands free. "I know you are worried, but I will be fine."

Her mother placed a hand on Hild's shoulder. "I am still not happy with you joining your brother on this trip. I have accepted, reluctantly, that Wilburh needs to go along to Vanaheim, but you don't, Hild. I don't want to lose both of you."

Hild frowned. "Oh, don't make a fuss. We are not planning to fight anyone. We are just talking to the Vanir. If the others are going then I am going too. I won't be left behind!"

"Well, still be careful, child. I will miss you." Juliana glanced over to where Wilburh, already packed and reading a scroll, was sitting on a bench. Lowering her voice, she said, "Oh, and watch over Wilburh, Hild. What he is messing around with is dangerous. I wish he would agree just to be a blacksmith."

"Would you rather I was just a blacksmith, Mother?"

Juliana blinked. "Of course not. You are a talented healer. That would be a waste of your abilities…" she trailed off as she realised Hild had tricked her. Wilburh had heard her and looked up at his twin, a slight smile on his lips.

"Wilburh does what he can do best, Mother," Hild said, firmly but softly. "This is where his talent lies. You should trust that he is doing the right thing." Blushing, Juliana nodded, but quickly returned to asking about Hild's potions.

Wilburh frowned at her and seemed about to say something, but then he just sighed, got up and walked towards the door.

Meccus and Ellette pushed past him, the small girl tottering along under the weight of the bundle on her back. Like all the children, she carried a pack similar to Hild's.

"Strike-a-light – where is your strike-a-light, Ellette?" Meccus asked.

"Father, I have it here – look, see?" She opened a pouch

hanging from her belt and pulled out the curved piece of iron and a fragment of flint to show him.

"Make sure you take enough arrows, Lar," Nerian ordered his son, having retired to his Headman's chair near the fire pit.

"Yes, Father." Lar held up a quiver of arrows to show he had at least thirty with him.

Nerian nodded and turned to Anna who was buckling on a scabbard. "Did you get that sword sharpened?" he demanded.

"It did not need sharpening," she said, showing him the blade.

"Are you sure?"

"It's true, Nerian," Meccus said, glancing across the Headsman's hut from where he was helping Ellette reorganise her pack. "I have examined the blade several times since the shield maiden returned with it and it holds its edge like no metal I have ever worked with or know of."

Leaning back in his chair, Nerian grunted in response.

"This pack is too heavy for you," Meccus said to his daughter, removing a flask of ale and a handful of apples and holding them out to Lar. "Have you got room for these?"

"Of course," Lar grinned. With a wink at Ellette, he leant across to take them, pushing them into his pack alongside his own.

Raising his eyebrows, Nerian returned his gaze to Anna's sword. "You are lucky, my girl, to own such a weapon. Bear it well, my daughter, and use it wisely to protect yourself, as well as those with you."

Anna studied her wonderful sword for a few moments then slid it back into the scabbard at her waist. "I will, Father," she answered quietly. Leaning against a bench was the new shield Meccus had given her. He must have worked through the night to finish it. She picked it up and passed her arms through the straps, testing its balance. She was pleased to find that it was both sturdy and at the same time light – just right for her. She became aware that her father was studying her anxiously.

"I am proud of you...of both of you," he added quickly with a glance at Lar, who seemed about to comment. "And so would your mother have been, if only she could see you now."

Sadness touched the Headsman's face, as it did whenever he thought of his wife who had died in a plague a year or so earlier. The same plague had taken many in the village, including Juliana's husband, Wilburh and Hild's father. For a time, stricken with grief Nerian had neglected his children, and Juliana had taken to mothering them. Although their father had eventually put his grief behind him, she still did. She eyed them now and was about to say something when a voice called from the doorway.

"You have good reason to be proud of them...of them all, in fact."

A figure stepped into the light at the entrance. He was tall, thin and elegant, dressed in a variety of mismatched clothes that were heavily darned and repaired. From his pack hung pans, tools, dried herbs, a smoked ham, some rather stale bread and a variety of trade goods.

"Raedann!" Anna shouted as he walked further into the hut.

A travelling storyteller, sometimes called bard or poet, Raedann was also a tinker, supplementing his income by buying and selling goods as he travelled from village to village recounting tales of the gods, monsters and battles.

He smiled at Anna. "I see I have arrived just in time. Where is that smelly old Dweorgar?"

"I am right behind you!"

Raedann spun round to see the dwarf glaring up at him, eyebrows bristling. "What was that about being smelly?" Gurthrunn growled.

"Just in time?" asked Anna, mostly to distract the grumpy dwarf. "In time for what, Raedann?"

"Your expedition. I got a message from Gurthrunn to say he was taking you with him to Vanaheim. He suggested I go along too in case you need someone with a silver tongue."

Gurthrunn scowled. "And I am regretting the idea already!"

Grinning at him, Raedann danced over to the tables, found a jug of mead and helped himself to it. "Here's to our expedition!" he toasted, lifting his mug up high. "I see you are packed, Anna, Lar, Hild, Ellette, but what about Wilburh? Where is he heading?"

They all looked towards the doorway. Wilburh had been lingering there, but was now scampering away.

"Where in Woden's name is the lad off to now?" Gurthrunn asked, staring after him.

Moments later Wilburh was standing in the doorway of Iden's temple, a shrine to the gods, which had been built in isolation on a small wooded hillock close by the village. It was where the priest led the villagers in worship. It was also where Wilburh was learning about the gods and their ways by listening to tales of their history and studying the runes – the ancient lettering that, alone out of the village children, Iden had taught him to read.

Peering into the gloom, Wilburh spotted the priest standing by the altar sorting through his scrolls. An overweight man in his fifties, Iden was bald with a round face and red cheeks. Although a strict tutor, he was neither harsh nor cruel, and Wilburh trusted him – trusted him enough to ask about something that had been occupying his mind since the skirmish with the ice elementals.

"Iden? Can you answer a question?"

"Be quick about it, then, you should be getting ready to leave."

"How does magic work?" Wilburh asked quickly.

Frowning, Iden looked up from his work. "What's that?"

"How does magic actually work? Can someone who uses it...lose the ability?"

The priest studied Wilburh for a while before answering. "My child, I am a priest of the gods. I know of them and of their ways, but I know little or no magic beyond simple blessings. I cannot...I cannot do what you do."

"But everything I know how to do I learnt from your scrolls," Wilburh pointed out, walking across the temple to stand next to his tutor. They both looked down at the scroll Iden had unrolled on the altar. The vellum was covered in runes that recorded the stories of the gods.

"Alas, the holy writings reveal knowledge to you that is hidden from me," Iden said with a sigh.

"So you don't know how magic works?"

"I know the Vanir gods use it and I can talk about when and why, but not *how*. All I can say is that I pray and use the rune sticks to call on the power of the gods – sticks like those I gave to you. Beyond that I really know nothing," the priest answered with a shake of his head.

Disconsolate, Wilburh started to turn away, but turned back when Iden spoke again. "One thing I do know, my son: while the Æsir gods have much power, they have little magic of their own. What magic they do have they learnt from the Vanir. You are travelling to Vanaheim. I would wager that you will have the best chance of finding an answer to your questions there. Good luck," he added with a kindly smile.

"Thank you." Wilburh nodded and walked out of the temple to see Lar hurrying up the wooded path towards him

"Ah, there you are. You had better get a move on, Wilburh. Gurthrunn is impatient to be off. You know how grumpy he can be. He keeps muttering, '*Does the boy not realise how important this is?*'"

Lar headed off back down the path, Wilburh plodding along behind. "I know how important it is, Lar, believe me I do," he said, adding under his breath, '*That is what bothers me.*'

He was still thinking about what Iden had said a short while later when they caught up with the others on their way to the barrow, the site of the previous day's battle. Aside from the grass being flattened in places and perhaps wetter than usual from the melted ice, there was otherwise no sign of what had happened there. The man standing guard nodded at them as Gurthrunn led the way up to the tomb at the top.

"Does it hurt?" Hild asked, gazing nervously at the doorway that opened onto the Bifrost. It was no longer plain stone slab as it had always appeared before the coming of Kendra earlier in the summer. Now it shimmered and moved like the sea, and had stripes with all the colours of the rainbow. Framing the portal was a stone arch engraved with runes that told of the Nine Worlds. Standing close to it they could all feel the energy flowing from this mystical gateway to other worlds.

The dwarf strapped his shield to his back and slipped his hammer into his belt so both arms were free, then he touched various runes in sequence, commanding the door, as he put it, to take them where he wished to go.

"Anna, does it hurt?" Hild asked again.

The shield maiden shook her head. "It is a little frightening and you might feel dizzy like I did the first time, but it doesn't hurt. Actually it is all over very quickly."

The dwarf turned to face them. "I am ready. Let us depart. I will lead the way, then the children will follow. Raedann, you come last," he instructed. Without any hesitation he stepped across the threshold, and in a flash of brilliant light vanished into the portal.

"Freya, protect me!" Hild gasped.

"It will be fine. Come, hang onto me," Anna said and held out her hand. Hild reached out and with shaking fingers grasped her friend's hand, holding on tight and closing her eyes as Anna led her through the Bifrost, Ellette on her heels.

Once the girls had gone, Lar turned to Raedann. "A copper piece for you to go next," he said.

Raedann laughed. "Make it four," he replied.

Shaking his head and knowing that Lar and Raedann

might haggle for a while, Wilburh strode past them towards the opening. As he hesitated at the threshold he could feel his hair standing up due to the pull of magic coming from the portal. Then he stepped in. His vision was filled with a swirling vortex of colours and lines. At first he shouted in terror as he spun head over heels through a whirlwind of magical forces so powerful he had never felt anything like it before. Then, after a moment he realised he could sense patterns in the chaos. More than that, he was certain that with a bit of effort he could direct his flight. Yes, he was convinced he would be able to ride the surging torrent as a sailor guides his vessel across heaving waters back to port. Then, abruptly, the journey was over and he was standing in a forest glade. Anna, Hild and Gurthrunn were all looking at him. Ellette was bouncing up and down, her cheeks flushed with excitement.

"You alright, son?" the gruff old dwarf asked.

Wilburh took a few deep breaths to clear his mind. "Yes...it's just quite a feeling, isn't it?"

"I felt sick the whole time," replied Hild, her face tinged green.

"I didn't," said Ellette.

Turning to look back at the Bifrost, Wilburh saw that at this end the opening was not in the arched doorway of a barrow like the one at Scenestane, but instead was framed by a pair of trees that had grown together so that their trunks curved and entwined, creating an arch-like gap in which the Bifrost shimmered. They stood about eight feet high, their trunks carved with the same runes that were engraved on the stone of the barrow doorway, which Gurthrunn had touched just before he vanished.

Lar emerged a few moments later, followed immediately by Raedann.

They all looked about them, examining their surroundings. Wilburh saw that his first impression that they were in a forest glade was not quite right. They were in fact standing on the top of a small hillock that was encircled by tall trees so that it resembled a huge crown. These trees grew far higher, possessed broader trunks and were covered with much greener leaves than those of the woods near Scenestane. A path led down from the hillock to a broad plain below them, which was dotted with occasional low hills surrounded in the distance by great mountains. The whole of the vast plain seemed filled with vineyards, farmland and meadows. Everywhere there were signs of fertile growth – fields of bulging fruit bushes, tall wheat stalks swaying gently or orchards laden with ripe red apples. Above them in sapphire-blue skies shone a sun, its heat just warm enough to be comfortable without making them sweat. At the base of the hill was a cluster of wooden halls and huts, similar to those they were used to but on a much larger scale.

As Gurthrunn led the way down the path towards them a sudden cool breeze blew across the tree tops and there was just a sprinkle of refreshing, cooling rain. Away in the distance Wilburh spotted a rainbow, its colours a faint replica of those in the Bifrost.

"The weather here seems perfect," Raedann commented.

Gurthrunn grunted. "That is no surprise. The Vanir are the gods of fertility, of living creatures and of all things that grow – of the winds and the rain and the harvest."

"It's very different from Asgard," Anna said, pointing at the buildings below them. "That was a huge city of towers and arches and massive stone temples."

"I wish I could have seen it," said Lar, envious of his sister's visit to Asgard back in the summer.

"The Vanir do not favour stone," Gurthrunn explained.

"They prefer their peace and quiet to the noise and bustle of the Æsir city. Their villages and halls are built of wood, more like those of your own people, whereas before you Angles came, the Romans did like their cities of stone, as I recall."

"Gurthrunn, the Romans left Britain 200 years ago, how could you remember?" Lar asked.

The dwarf shrugged. "We Dweorgar may not be immortal, but we do live a long time – much longer than your kind."

"I said he was old," Raedann pointed out, "smelly *and* old, in fact!"

Gurthrunn bristled again and looked ready to start up on the previous day's argument when Wilburh distracted them.

"This is an odd place," he observed.

They had now reached an open space between a dozen large wooden halls, each topped with thatched roofing. As they looked about them, Wilburh noticed that there was not a soul to be seen – not one inhabitant anywhere in sight. Nor, barring the distant trill of birds, was there a sound to be heard.

"There is perhaps such a thing as too much peace and quiet," he commented.

Gurthrunn, looking anxious, had apparently noticed the same thing.

"Something is very wrong here," he said.

# CHAPTER FIVE

## TROLL!

"Where is everyone?" Lar asked.

In answer the Dweorgar simply shook his head, and then, as his gaze wandered over the buildings around them, he stiffened. In a blur he brought his huge war hammer down from his shoulder, holding it out at the ready position.

"Prepare yourselves, it's an ambush!" he hissed, tilting his head towards a gap between two halls.

The others now peered in the direction he was indicating. The alleyway was cast in shadow and at first they could see nothing. Frowning at their blank faces, Gurthrunn pointed again at whatever his dwarven eyes, superbly adapted for seeing well in dark passageways, were showing him.

They all stared into the shadows, and this time Ellette gasped. "I see them! Svartálfar, hiding in the shadows! What are *they* doing here? I see a dozen at least," she said, pulling her sling from her belt. In an instant she had retrieved a handful of pebbles from her pouch and held them clutched in one hand.

"There too," Lar said, pointing at another space between what seemed to be a huge barn and a smithy standing on the other side of the green. He strung his bow and in a flash had an arrow notched on the string. Anna and Raedann drew swords and Hild her own sling.

Wilburh brought out his rune sticks and gave them a dubious glare. Why had they failed him the day before? he asked himself. Would they work this time?

"Do we want to get out of the open and find somewhere to defend – a doorway, maybe?" Anna suggested.

Gurthrunn nodded. "Agreed, but let's move quickly," he replied, heading towards the barn.

Before they got very far a guttural cry came from the first group of Svartálfar, taken up in a moment by all those that had suddenly appeared on both sides of them.

Then the dark elves attacked.

As they charged out into the sunlight, Anna and her companions recognised the creatures as those they had fought so hard against earlier in the year when Kendra's army of elves had attacked Scenestane. Svartálfar might only be about the same height as Ellette, but they had proved nasty and vicious enemies.

"Use your bow, Lar. Ellette, prepare your sling. Get ready!" Gurthrunn yelled.

The elves spread out and surged across the open green, all of them screaming or snarling, showing their sharp pointed teeth. Thrusting with their short javelins or slashing out with the curved blades of their cruel looking scimitars, the dark little creatures threatened the six companions as they backed away.

An arrow leapt from Lar's bow, hitting a dark elf squarely in the chest. The creature screeched as it collapsed. He fired again and again, and two more went down. Ellette's sling was whirling around her head, and then with a flick of the wrist she released the stone. It spun tumbling through the air and bounced off a snarling dark elf who crumpled to the ground. She reloaded and let fly again. Now five dark elves were down, but fifty more were hurtling towards the companions.

Wilburh focused on his rune sticks and clutched them nervously in his sweaty palm. He saw Anna crane her head to glance at him, wondering why he did not act perhaps, and so he stared intently at the small pieces of wood, each engraved with runes that were meant to summon power into the hands of the wielder. They had worked before when he had forced the snake to back away the day they had found the gold horn in the ruined villa. Later on that same night he had used them again when the barghests, monstrous black dogs, had attacked, and he had used them to great effect during the Battle of Scenestane. So surely they would serve him again now?

He stepped out in front of Anna, lifted up his hands and, holding them out towards the dark elves, shouted, "*Sunne Ablaedan!*"

He felt warmth pass from the sticks into his hands, saw his hands begin to glow, thrust them out towards the snarling creatures, and then...the glow just went out, the warmth faded away and he was left standing in front of a horde of Svartálfar who were now just ten paces away.

"I don't understand..." he said, looking down at his hands.

"Get back, boy!" Gurthrunn roared as he seized Wilburh by the neck of his tunic and tugged him backwards. He whirled round and then tripped, ending up on all fours, looking down at the rune sticks which were knocked out of his hands as he fell. "I don't understand," he repeated.

An arrow from Lar and a stone – this time from Hild – knocked two more dark elves down, and then the creatures had arrived in front of them.

"*Nidarvellir!*" Gurthrunn bellowed his traditional Dweorgar battle cry and heaved his huge war hammer in a circle that smashed into four of the elves, sending them tumbling away as if they weighed no more than a child's doll.

One of them snarled and threw a javelin at Anna. She brought up her shield and the missile bounced off and hurtled over their heads. Then she stepped forward a half pace and thrust the point of her sword at the creature. The dark elf was clad in a light chain shirt, but Anna's sword, which gave off a high-pitched hum as she wielded it, sliced through the metal rings as if they were mere sheaves of wheat under a farmer's scythe. The blade dug deep into the dark elf's shoulder and the creature crumpled and fell. Anna brought her sword back to parry the attack of the next foe. By her side, Raedann danced lightly from foot to foot, using his speed and agility to dodge the dark elf attacks then nipping forward to deliver a cut or thrust, before whirling away again, pots and pans clattering on his pack.

Ellette and Lar were shooting stones and arrows over the shoulders of Gurthrunn and Anna while they and Raedann used their swords to keep the dark elves at bay. With so many Svartálfar now wounded or dead, it seemed that the attack was failing, for the creatures had yet to inflict any real injury upon the companions. Meanwhile, on the ground behind Gurthrunn, Wilburh was still on his hands and knees, staring in disbelief at the rune sticks.

"Are you hurt?" Hild asked him, crouching by his side.

He looked up and could tell from her expression that she knew he was not, but was not sure how to ask the question that was on her mind: *What is wrong with Wilburh and his magic?*

Shaking his head at his twin, Wilburh pulled himself to his feet. He stared again at the sticks, and then after a moment bent to pick them up and put them away in his belt pouch. He drew his seax and moved to the left side of Gurthrunn, where two dark elves were trying to come round the side of the Dweorgar and get in a position to attack him from flank or rear. The dwarf glanced Wilburh's way, frowned at the blade in the boy's hand, but turned back to the battle without comment.

Despite Wilburh's personal difficulties, the battle was going well. Gurthrunn grunted with effort as he once again swung with his war hammer and the huge weapon pulverised another three Svartálfar. Raedann and Anna were working together now, covering each other as they moved back and forth, darting forward to stab the Svartálfar and then retreating away from their vicious blades. On either side, Ellette's pebbles and Lar's arrows were taking their toll of any dark elves who tried to spread out and encircle them. Even Hild and Wilburh were contributing by protecting the archer and slinger from any that came too close.

It seemed then that the Svartálfar had decided they were getting nowhere because the vicious little creatures started to pull back. Ellette, obviously feeling that she and her companions had won, laughed and cheered.

Then something huge stepped out onto the green and Ellette's mouth dropped open.

It was a monster: three times the height of Raedann and four times that of the children and dwarf. Its arms and legs were as thick as tree trunks, and as it moved the ground shook beneath its feet. The monster's skin was grey-green and the half-dozen teeth, visible when it opened its mouth to roar, were yellow. With an angry red eye it fixed its gaze on them and stumbled forward in a lolloping gait, a massive club clutched in its huge, knobbly hands. The dark elves parted to let this beast through, and then rallied behind it and came on in its wake.

"Troll!" Gurthrunn yelled as he stepped forward to stand in the beast's path.

Before the troll was close enough to Gurthrunn for him to hit it, the monster's enormous arms allowed it to swing the great club down at the dwarf. He tried to leap to one side, but the club head was a rock as big as he was and it simply hammered the Dweorgar warrior into the ground.

"Gurthrunn!" Anna screamed, but the dwarf lay unmoving and did not respond. The troll leapt over its fallen

prey, thumped onto the green with an impact that sent shock waves through the earth and came running on towards them.

For a long moment none of the companion said anything. They were all frozen to the spot in shock and horror: stunned by what they had just seen.

"I think he's dead," Raedann shouted, staring at the Dweorgar's body. Then he looked up at the huge form of the troll looming down upon him. "Run, children, run!" he screamed.

With the tinker waving them on, run they did, aiming to reach the Bifrost. If they could get there and travel through it they would reach Midgard, their own village and safety. But as they turned and fled, they only made it two dozen paces before the Svartálfar, scampering across the grass, overtook them and cut them off. They all drew to a halt and the dark elves spread out around them, encircling them.

"You have lost! Drop your weapons!" one of the dark elves screeched at them in the high-pitched voices they had. He was larger than his fellows – a captain, maybe.

The children hesitated.

The captain elf stepped forward and, drawing his scimitar, pointed at Gurthrunn. "The Dweorgar is dead. Drop your weapons at once or we will kill the rest of you!" he ordered.

# CHAPTER SIX

## GLEIPNIR

Anna took a few steps back towards where Gurthrunn lay unmoving on the grass, but the dark elf captain scuttled over to her, snarled at her and then screamed, "Get back, leave him!" Anna glared at the creature and tightened her grip on her sword as she brought the weapon back, preparing to use it again.

Seeing the movement, the Svartálfar screamed at her again, "Drop your weapons now, or I will command the troll to kill you all!"

"Anna, do as he says, we can't win. Not today," Raedann said, throwing his own sword to the ground.

She turned, preparing to argue with the tinker. Her sword was named 'Aefre', which meant 'forever'. It was not just any old sword, but one of great beauty and strength. It had been handed to her personally by the God of all gods, and it pained her greatly to give it up.

"I *can't*," she hissed.

"You *must*," Raedann said out of the corner of his mouth, his gaze on the advancing troll.

She hesitated a moment longer, then she sighed, her shoulders sagged and she gave in. With a venomous glare at the dark elf captain, she dropped Aefre at her feet.

The others now followed suit, dropped their swords,

52

knives and slings, and Lar his bow, then huddling together, they gazed fearfully at the Svartálfar. The creatures came forward, stripped them of their packs and flung them with Raedann's various possessions in a heap on the ground, then collected up all their weapons. It took three of them to lift Gurthrunn's huge hammer. Next, the children and Raedann were forced to stand with their arms in front of them while the Svartálfar bound their wrists together and then tied each of them to a long rope.

The troll was examining Gurthrunn.

"Well," asked the captain, "is he dead?"

The monster sniffed at the dwarf and then prodded him viciously.

"Leave him be!" shouted Anna.

"You shut up!" the captain snarled. With a glare at Anna, he turned back to the troll. "Well, does he live?"

"He lives" was the grunted response, accompanied by a slow nod of the great head. "You want me to kill him?"

"He's alive?" Lar asked in relief.

"I said be silent! I could order him killed right now, and I will if you don't shut up," the captain snapped.

The troll lifted its club a few feet. "You want me to kill?" it repeated eagerly.

The Svartálfar captain waited a moment before replying, obviously enjoying watching the children's faces as they stared at the troll in horror.

"No. Do not kill. Not yet," he said finally.

With a look of disappointment, the troll stared down at Gurthrunn, and it took another snapped order from the captain before it slowly lowered its club.

"Come on then, we are going." The captain barked out an order to the dark elves, and then turned back to the troll. "Bring the Dweorgar."

"Now what?" asked Anna, glaring at the Svartálfar's leader.

"Now you come with us" was the simple answer. He turned on his heel and led the way, followed by the dark elves, their prisoners trailing along behind. The troll bent over, picked up Gurthrunn, tossed him over its shoulder as if the dwarf was no larger than a baby, then stomped along in their wake.

They marched towards the largest of the halls on the far side of the grassy lawn. Wilburh looked around him with interest, noting that the lintel over the door frame was marked with a variety of runes, each a symbol of a Vanir God, he assumed. The doors themselves were decorated with elaborate carvings of beasts of the earth, sea and air, as well as many that were unfamiliar to him – creatures from other worlds, perhaps. As they approached the hall he realised that the building was even bigger than he had at first thought; it was actually *massive*. Wilburh estimated that the entire village of Scenestane would fit inside it. In fact it looked in many ways like an impossibly vast version of Nerian's Headman's hall. He muttered something about this to Raedann.

"Well, the Vanir might favour simpler structures to the massive stone halls that Anna described from her trip to Asgard," the tinker said, "but they are still gods, and gods just do everything on a larger scale than us mere mortals."

When they arrived at the entrance, the dark elf captain pushed open the enormous pair of doors, which swung inwards to reveal a many-pillared hall. Supported on these huge columns, which resembled the trunks of massive trees, the cavernous roof was a full fifty feet above them. As they walked down the centre of the room, past the twin rows of pillars, they could see fires burning in circular pits between each one. Attached to the pillars were sconces holding flaming torches that cast flickering shadows in the hall. It seemed to go on forever, and much like the green outside, it seemed in places to stretch as they got closer to it. What had appeared from a distance to be a small village of human proportions – albeit with larger buildings than they were used to – took on a much more divine scale when examined close up.

"There is powerful magic at work here," Wilburh said.

"You can feel it?" Lar asked him.

Wilburh shrugged. "More than feel it. It is as if we are swimming through it. It is all around us."

The end of the hall had appeared distant, almost out of sight, but as they drew closer they could see a set of huge wooden thrones arrayed in a semi-circle at the far end. "We seem to be inside a throne room," Wilburh muttered. "Perhaps it's an audience chamber where the Vanir gods hold court."

Lar didn't respond. Like the others, he was craning his neck, eager for his first sight of these gods they had come to visit. Yet as they neared, disappointingly each of the thrones was empty.

Each of them, that was, except one.

Reclining in decadent elegance upon a throne, waited on by half a dozen Svartálfar, each holding trays of food or jugs of refreshments, was none other than the fallen Valkyrie, their bitter enemy and the cause of all their woes.

Kendra!

Each of the children and even the usually unflappable Raedann stopped abruptly in their tracks and just stood gawping. Obviously irritated by the delay, the Svartálfar escorting them tugged on the rope and snarled. The captain snapped out a command and two of the dark elves produced whips, which they now cracked in the air then flicked at Raedann and Lar so that the lashes stung their backs. Others pushed at the children from behind or prodded them with knife points so that soon they were off again, stumbling along towards the throne. All the while Kendra sat in silence, glaring at the prisoners.

Finally they arrived in front of her. The dark elves parted, and they were left standing mere yards from the occupied throne. Gurthrunn was deposited on the ground near their feet – still unconscious and unmoving.

For a long time the sorceress gazed at them and said nothing, as though she were considering them each in turn. Finally, tall, graceful and extraordinarily beautiful, she rose to her feet, descended from her throne and walked slowly over to them.

"So, you come again into my presence: you who did so much to destroy my designs on Midgard. At last I have you in my power. How marvellous the fate which delivered you to me." She drew a short knife from a scabbard at her belt. "Indeed I could take great pleasure in killing each of you myself, one by one, here and now...especially *you*..." she hissed as the knife point moved closer to Anna's throat.

Anna froze, not daring to move.

Raedann stepped forward, straining against the rope. "Leave her be!" he commanded.

Smirking at him, Kendra shrugged, and with a flash returned the blade to its home. "Your deaths can wait. I have just had a far better idea of what to do with you all. Come with me," and crooking her finger, she marched away from them.

Leaving the unconscious Gurthrunn, who was lying on the ground guarded by the troll, Raedann and the children were prodded along by the spears and blades of the dark elves. The Valkyrie led them behind the thrones to a door set into the rear wall. It opened into a room furnished with finely upholstered couches, chairs and tables. The walls were hung with tapestries and friezes depicting warriors fighting each other, or the gods out hunting in the forest. Between the tables there were many tall cabinets consisting of little niches and shelves in which were deposited scrolls of parchment – hundreds of them, maybe even thousands. Several were open on a nearby table, and the children could see that these were covered in runes and fine illustrations in vibrant colours. Radeann's face took on an expression of awe.

"Merciful Woden, it's a library!" he exclaimed.

Captivated by the sight of them, Wilburh felt an overwhelming urge to rush over and start reading the scrolls; an urge he would have been unable to resist had he not been roped to his companions. Surely somewhere among those parchments lay the wisdom and knowledge he needed. Here must be the answer to his problems with magic as well as to the needs of the village itself. He noticed the other children glancing at them then looking away with little sign of any further interest. He sighed. None of the others, of course, could read, and to them the power of the runes – almost magic by themselves – and the meanings of the words meant nothing. He exchanged glances with Raedann and they shared a moment of wonder.

Enchanted as he was by the beauty of the scrolls and the staggering thought of so many in one place – after all, Iden possessed only a meagre half dozen – Wilburh had failed to notice for a moment what his companions had shifted their attention to, but now his eyes widened as he saw what that was.

Lying on the couches, or else on the ground between them, were twelve figures. As soon as he laid eyes on them,

Wilburh knew that these were gods. Not just because of their great height and build, but because there was something about their presence, some power to their personality that instantly identified them as immortal: ancient, and at the same time eternally young. Six were male and six female, and all of them were bound hand and foot and also had gags around their mouths. Twenty-four eyes were shut, and it seemed as if the gods were in fact asleep.

"The Vanir…?" Anna gasped.

With a smirk, the sorceress nodded. "Indeed. I, Kendra, have captured and bound them. They are harmless thus imprisoned. Not even their fabled magic can help them now."

"But how? How was this done?" Raedann asked.

Kendra frowned. "How did I capture them or how are they held?"

"Both, I guess," the tinker replied.

58

She shrugged. "In either event, it is the same answer: *Gleipnir!*"

His face blanching white as chalk, Raedann gasped, "How did you get hold of *that*?"

The sorceress blinked. "I am Kendra," she answered, as if that was enough of an explanation in itself.

"What is Gleipnir?" Anna asked Raedann.

"The chain that binds the great wolf Fenrir until Ragnarok comes" was his answer. Anna seemed none the wiser, and Raedann opened his mouth to expand on the explanation.

"Answers can wait for now," Kendra snapped. "I am sure the shield maiden would prefer a more direct demonstration. Let me show you."

Swift as a striking snake, she cut the rope at Raedann's wrists and pushed him away from the children. Almost in the same movement she reached into a pouch at her belt and brought out what appeared to be a thin golden thread on a silver spindle. Before Raedann could react, Kendra, clutching one end of the thread, tossed the rest towards him. Unravelling from the spindle, it flew across the gap between them, but instead of dropping to the ground, when it reached Raedann the thread latched onto his left wrist and then whipped around his body, tugging his arm with it. He cried out in alarm and pain, trying to get away, but in a blur, as if it had a life of its own, the thread coiled around his waist – two, three, five, ten times – and then moved down to spin around his legs. With a shout he tumbled over and crashed to the ground. The length binding him then parted from the rest, which coiled itself around the spindle and returned gently to Kendra's hand. She smiled and put the Gleipnir thread back in her pouch.

"Let me go!" Raedann demanded, rolling around and

struggling on the ground at her feet.

"I will let you go when the children do exactly as I say, and not before," Kendra said.

Suddenly defiant, Anna faced their captor. "And what if we won't?"

Kendra laughed. "If you do not I will have the Svartálfar cut the tinker's throat and then yours, and this library will be your tomb forever!"

# Chapter Seven

## The Task

Sweat stood out on Raedann's brow as, grunting and puffing, he fought against the golden thread wrapped around his wrists and ankles. He was not as strong as Gurthrunn, but was still a powerful man, and yet the bonds held fast. Kendra, amused, watched him struggle.

"Come now, Master Bard, you surely know full well the tales of Gleipnir, and yet you struggle so. You must know it is futile!"

After rolling around for a few moments more, Raedann gave up the fight, slumped back on the ground and lay still. Then he lifted his head, craning his neck to look up at Kendra.

"You have me bound, sorceress, but let the children go and I will do whatever you wish."

Breaking into laughter, she gazed down at him. "What makes you think I want *you*: a tinker, a penniless poet, a vagabond wanderer? I care nothing for you. You are bound because having you as my prisoner will force these children and the cursed Dweorgar to do exactly what I ask of them." She snapped her fingers at two dark elves and pointed at Anna and her companions. "Untie them."

The creatures scuttled to do her bidding. As the rope fell away, the children rubbed at their wrists and eyed each other grimly. They all knew that without weapons, greatly outnumbered by the dark elves and with Raedann in the Valkyrie's power, any attempt at running away would be pointless. As if to confirm it, Kendra gestured at the tinker and smiled.

"If any of you makes a move to escape, he dies. Understand?" Her smile was evil.

They nodded.

At that moment a shape appeared in the doorway. The

children turned to look. Gurthrunn was standing there, hands tied behind his back, his face bruised, swollen and bloody. He was being dragged into the room by the troll. The dwarf took in the forms of the bound and gagged Vanir and a look of outrage sprang to his face. Then he focussed on the Valkyrie and the outrage changed to murderous fury.

"Kendra!" Gurthrunn shouted. Wrenching himself free of the troll's arms, he jumped forward and then gave a cry, tripped over and ended up sprawled on the ground.

Wilburh, at first relieved to see that Gurthrunn was apparently not seriously wounded, now noticed that as well as his wrists, the Dweorgar's ankles were shackled.

Gurthrunn rolled over and hauled himself into a crouch. He stared angrily up at Kendra, his mouth working but no words coming out.

"Ah, the Dweorgar joins us, we are truly blessed," she mocked, a sarcastic smile on her lips. "You have arrived just in time to receive my orders. You will obey them if you wish to see your friend the tinker alive again."

"Obey *you*, you traitor? I will *never* obey you," Gurthrunn growled.

Kendra clicked her fingers and in an instant the Svartálfar captain bent over Raedann, a curved dagger touching the skin at the tinker's throat.

The dwarf glared at Kendra, but after a moment, with a glance at the white-faced children, he slowly nodded. "Very well, Valkyrie. I am compelled to obey you...for now."

"The sooner you accept that I am going to win once and for all, the better. You will save yourself much trouble this way, dwarf."

Gurthrunn grunted. "We shall see. Now tell me what it is you want of us and be done with it!"

With a self-satisfied smirk, Kendra nodded. "You as a Dweorgar will be familiar with the catacombs beneath the Vanir halls, I assume."

The dwarf looked surprised, then shrugged. "I am aware of them. I am hardly familiar. They were built an age ago and I have never seen them."

"Catacombs? What catacombs are those, Gurthrunn?" Lar asked, a worried frown creasing his brow.

"You might as well tell the boy," Kendra said. "He and his companions will be coming with you."

"Them too?"

"Indeed." Kendra nodded.

"But it is dangerous…"

"They either accompany you or die here. Besides, even I will acknowledge that despite their young years they fought well at that cursed village on Midgard. They are capable, and you might fail alone."

"What is she talking about?" Anna demanded, looking first at Gurthrunn and then at Kendra.

"The Catacombs of Vanaheim," Gurthrunn replied, glancing over at the dormant forms of the gods, still bound and immobile, apparently sleeping, but he knew it was not a normal sleep. He took a deep breath. "Let me explain. The Vanir are powerful weavers of magic and rune lore. In partnership with my own people, they created great treasures. Most of the treasures of the gods were made here, in the smithies and workshops that are housed in the other buildings outside the hall.

"Treasures like Heimdall's horn?" Wilburh asked.

"Exactly like that, yes, and more besides. The gods, anxious that their creations would fall into the wrong hands, like those of the Svartálfar maybe, or even Loki himself, took steps to preserve the safety of these precious items.

They had my people dig out a labyrinth of passageways – for above all, we dwarves are unsurpassed at creating tunnels and chambers in bare rock – and in that maze, which lies deep beneath our feet, they store their treasures."

"A maze, is that all? Surely the treasures would be found in the end?" Wilburh suggested.

Gurthrunn nodded. "Yes. You are quite correct. So a maze would not be enough. The catacombs were filled with traps and monsters to make a journey through them very hazardous indeed. Finally, as a defence mechanism they cannot be entered by an immortal, whether it be a god, a Valkyrie or a dark elf, or indeed any other being that is not mortal. They can be entered only by those who possess a mortal soul, such as dwarves. When my ancestors built the catacombs for the gods, they made them so that only the Dweorgar, who alone could be trusted with its secrets, would be able to enter."

Anna looked over at the Valkyrie, who was listening to the explanation but looking a bit bored. Anna thrust out a finger towards her. "So *she* is after something. She wants a treasure from down there, but she can't go, nor can her servants the dark elves, so she wants us to do it for her." Anna frowned. "Wait a moment, though. If the gods cannot go down there, who would normally fetch up an item they need?"

"That's a good question," said Gurthrunn. "In fact the Vanir have a number of my people here, those who moved to Vanaheim to build the catacombs and then stayed on to serve the Vanir gods. In effect they protected the treasures and became the stewards and guardians, as did their descendants after them." Gurthrunn's face became quizzical. "I wonder why she has not tried to force them to get whatever it is that she wants. Then again, perhaps she has. Whatever her threats, they would refuse her. The gods knew what they were doing when they employed dwarves in their service. We Dweorgar would rather die than yield."

Kendra scowled, and from her expression it seemed Gurthrunn was correct. "How stubborn a race you dwarves are!" she hissed. "Yes, those who serve the Vanir have refused to obey me. Some I killed. The others escaped me and retreated into the catacombs. They will not fetch the treasures, so you will have to – you and the children."

"Wait a moment, how can we go?" Anna asked Gurthrunn. "I thought it was only dwarves."

He shook his head. "When the dwarves made the catacomb impassable to those without a mortal soul, I imagine it never occurred to them that ordinary mortals like you would ever find their way to Vanaheim, but..."

He broke off as Kendra, becoming suddenly impatient, snapped her fingers. "Enough of your explanations, Dweorgar. You will all go, save for the bard who I will keep as a hostage to guarantee your return."

"Very well," Anna said. "Assuming we do not get killed in the process, what items would you have us fetch for you?"

"I want two items. Firstly, you will locate a cloak made of falcon feathers."

Wilburh gasped as a flash of memory came to him – something he had read in one of Iden's scrolls. "Freya's cloak?" he asked.

Kendra glanced at him. "You have heard of the item? You are more knowledgeable than I would have expected for a child of Midgard. Yes, I desire her cloak. Although she dwells now in Asgard, Freya is a Vanir by birth and it is here where her cloak is kept."

"Very well. What other item do you want us to fetch for you?" Gurthrunn demanded.

"A clay pot about so big," Kendra replied, holding her hands out to indicate the size. "It is about the same height and width as a large cook pot and is engraved with the M rune."

"What is this pot?" Anna asked.

"It does not matter what it is. Do not try to open it. You would fail anyway – it can be opened only by a god..." she smirked "...or perhaps a powerful sorceress."

Gurthrunn frowned. "I see. So when are we to start?"

The Valkyrie opened her lips to reply, but Wilburh, who had been following the conversation closely, found he could not hear her. It was as if the world had fallen suddenly silent. He could see Kendra pacing around the room speaking, and Gurthrunn nodding and then asking some other questions, yet Wilburh could hear neither the sound of Kendra's footsteps nor a word from either of them. He stared at them in bewilderment. For a moment he wondered if Kendra and Gurthrunn were playing a trick on the rest of them, but realised at once how preposterous an idea that was. They were hardly close friends given to concocting elaborate jokes, as Lar and Raedann were prone to do. On the contrary, they were bitter enemies. Moreover, the rest of the children could obviously hear what was going on because he had just noticed Anna was saying something, and Hild, nodding in agreement, was responding. Even little Ellette was now speaking; he could see her lips moving, but again heard no sound.

*Merciful gods, I am deaf,* he thought, popping one finger in each ear and checking for wax.

"*You are not deaf, child of Midgard. Forgive the intrusion, but I needed to speak to you,*" a voice replied inside his head. Wilburh looked around at the other children, but they were paying attention to Kendra and did not seem to have heard the other voice.

He shook his head. *Not deaf. Mad then. I am going mad*, Wilburh thought.

"*You are not mad either,*" the voice replied with a hint of amusement. "*I am really speaking to you. I chose you as you are the one with the most power, and it is that power that makes this possible.*"

Wilburh now wondered if it was the owner of the other voice who was going mad for thinking he had power. "Whoever you are, I don't have much power, I am afraid," he whispered softly.

"Yes you do, but we don't have time to argue about it. You don't need to speak out loud, just think what you want to say. I can hear your thoughts. But you do need to listen carefully to what I am about to tell you."

# CHAPTER EIGHT

## ULLR

"Who…what are you?" Wilburh asked in his thoughts.

He stood behind the others who were examining a map that Kendra had produced. From what he could see, peering over their shoulders, it seemed to portray a maze-like set of passageways: the catacombs, presumably. The Valkyrie was standing to one side, her gaze on the Dweorgar.

"*I am the God Ullr. I am lying over here near the golden table,*" said the voice in Wilburh's head. He looked quickly at Kendra, certain she must have heard, but she was now saying something to Gurthrunn and not looking in Wilburh's direction.

"*Do not worry, the sorceress cannot hear us,*" said Ullr.

Reassured, Wilburh edged backwards and cast his gaze around the room, searching the dormant forms of the gods and goddesses that lay unmoving beneath the tables and upon the couches. Then he spotted one god lying near a table with golden runes engraved upon it. He was a tall, handsome god with powerful muscles visible in his bare upper arms. But what drew Wilburh's attention was not the god's physical strength so much as the bright, attentive eyes that were even now gazing at him. The other gods were apparently asleep, or at least unconscious, but this god, unique among all of them, was not only awake but alert – and looking right at him.

"Yes, *that is me*," said the god. It was an odd voice. Young with life and vigour, but at the same time it also had an edge to it that spoke of ancient wisdom.

"What is happening?" Wilburh asked, sidling nearer to the table.

"*My kin are sleeping. I alone am conscious, and in my case not for much longer. I am using your power to talk to you.*"

"You can't be. I told you I don't have the power. It has failed me."

"*No it has not. You will find that out before this is over. But we must hurry. A few days ago Kendra caught us gods by surprise, one by one, and bound us with Gleipnir. I was the last to be caught as I was out hunting in the mountains far from here. What do you know of Gleipnir?*"

Wilburh considered what he knew of the legends. "Our priest told me that Gleipnir was a thread made to trap the great wolf Fenrir, the chief and most powerful of all wolves. The beast was rampaging around Asgard. No one could control it, not even a god, until Tiw, the Warrior God, made a bargain. He agreed to put his hand in Fenrir's great jaws to distract the wolf while the other gods created a magic thread to bind the creature and render it harmless. The wolf was secured, but that deal cost Tiw his hand, which is why all images of Tiw show him with just one hand. His bravery made him the god that most warriors worship."

*"I am impressed by your knowledge. It surprises me that the goings on of us gods are known in mortal Midgard,"* said Ullr.

Wilburh nodded to himself. "To some of us they are known, and this tale better than most. The gods could not contain the ravenous wolf, so Gleipnir was made by the dwarves to secure it, and it is now trapped along with its master, Loki, the Trickster God, until the end of time."

*"Indeed, or trapped until someone should let them go. But enough of that, the point is that Kendra was able to steal some of the thread and use it to trap us Vanir. Bound by it we cannot move and cannot use magic, and the longer one remains bound by it, the more subdued one becomes, until eventually slumber follows, and then sleep from which it is impossible to wake without the intervention of powerful magic. That is what has happened to my kin – the other gods. Only I – the last to be trapped – remain awake, and even now I can feel the golden thread working its power and slumber coming upon me too."*

"I don't understand, how can I help you? I don't have powerful magic. I don't have any magic at all..." Wilburh faltered.

*"Yes, you do, but I don't have time to explain. The thread is taking my mind. Kendra knew this would be a way to overcome us. But there is a way you can help...a way to sever Gleipnir."*

Kendra was folding the map and looking about her. Wilburh swiftly averted his gaze for fear she would see what had caught his attention, but he still could not hear what was being said, though he could see Gurthrunn was speaking as he turned to the children. The other four moved towards the door, leaving Wilburh standing alone near Ullr's table. Gurthrunn looked over at him with a puzzled expression and said something, which again Wilburh could not hear. He tried to speak and say he was coming, but from the expression on Gurthrunn's face he had not made any sound. Kendra now turned her head to fix Wilburh with a suspicious glare.

"Lord Ullr, tell me quickly what I must do. Kendra is looking at me."

*"Yes, I know...it's just that I am feeling sleepy and I can't concentrate, Gleipnir is taking me..."*

Out of the corner of his eye, Wilburh could see Ullr was blinking, obviously trying to fight the sleep that was rapidly overwhelming him.

Kendra began walking towards Wilburh, staring straight at him.

"Hurry, Lord Ullr, please! How can we help you?"

*"You must fetch something...if only I could remember..."* Ullr's eyes had closed.

The sorceress was now right in front of Wilburh, bending forward so she was almost nose to nose with him.

"Please, Lord Ullr!" Wilburh pleaded.

*"I have remembered...the sword, Gambantein. You must bring me Gambantein, it..."*

Then the presence in Wilburh's mind was gone, and suddenly the sounds of the world about him rushed back into his head with an abruptness that made him dizzy, sending him staggering to one side. He reached out and caught hold of a chair to steady himself.

"What is wrong with you, boy?" Kendra demanded.

Wilburh stared at her. "What?"

"I said, WHAT IS WRONG WITH YOU?" Kendra roared.

Now Gurthrunn and the other children were all staring at him.

"Nothing...nothing. I just felt dizzy, that is all."

Kendra leant even closer and looked him in the eye. "That is all? Are you certain? If I find out you have lied to me then I will kill you myself."

"What else could it be?" Wilburh said grumpily. "I don't feel well."

"Very well, you'll just have to pull yourself together, boy. This is enough time wasted. Now come!" The sorceress whirled round and stomped towards the door.

With a last glance at the now sleeping Ullr, Wilburh followed. As he walked along behind Kendra, Lar came across and leant close to him. "What was that all about?"

Wilburh shook his head. "I can't tell you now. Ask me later," he whispered.

They all trailed after Kendra back through the audience chamber and then into the world outside. Gurthrunn, who was still shackled, shuffled along supported by the troll. They were led around the back of the great hall towards a low hill that rose out of the earth behind it. The hill was mostly covered in grass, rather like the barrow at Scenestane, but set into the side, facing the rear of the god's hall, was a pair of enormous wooden doors. Each of them bore a huge brass ring. Fifty Svartálfar were guarding this entrance.

73

Although it was quiet at present, there had clearly been a battle here recently, for on the ground in front of the doors lay several dead bodies, three of them dwarves. These were the first dwarves the children had seen other than their friend Gurthrunn. They all looked to have been every bit as powerful and strong as he: all were armoured in steel chain shirts and helmets, their lifeless hands still clutching giant war hammers. The Dweorgar had obviously given the Svartálfar a fierce fight: there were no fewer than twenty dark elves lying dead all around them.

Glancing down at the slain dwarves, Kendra remarked to Gurthrunn, "Your people died in vain – the fools."

He looked sadly at the bodies of his kin. "These Dweorgar were guardians, they died doing what they swore to do. They died with honour. But you, a creature with no honour, would not understand that."

"Perhaps not," Kendra sniffed. "However, I do understand one thing: they died because they refused to give me access to the artefacts I desire. Their companions – more of the same fools – retreated behind these doors. They are somewhere within. They would not hand me the items I asked for. They are your problem now. You must persuade them to comply with my demands or else the bard dies," Kendra said, holding out the map of the catacombs.

"You will have to untie my bonds if you want me to take that," Gurthrunn said. "And while you're at it, give us back our weapons. Without them we would last no longer than a snowflake in the fire world Muspelheim!"

She glared at him, but after a moment she nodded at a group of the Svartálfar, who came forward and deposited all of the children's belongings – their packs, weapons and shields, along with Gurthrunn's war hammer – upon the ground at their feet. Then Kendra clicked her fingers at the troll, who in one movement of its giant hands ripped apart the dwarf's shackles.

Rubbing at his wrists and ankles, Gurthrunn glowered at the troll, then picking up his war hammer and shield, he took the map, thrust it inside his chain shirt and, without a word, turned away and stomped towards the huge wooden doors.

Hastily grabbing up their things, the children followed. "She has a point, doesn't she?" Lar asked, shrugging into the straps of his pack as he scuttled along behind the dwarf, his bow and quiver carried over one shoulder. "How are we going to get the dwarves to give us the treasures?"

"My people are stubborn. It will not be easy," Gurthrunn said.

"You are so encouraging. You know that, don't you."

Gurthrunn stared at the boy. "Never mind about the Dweorgar, lad. They will protect the treasure chamber. If we get that far then we will deal with them."

"If we get that far?" said Hild. "What do you mean, *if* we get that far?" She looked across nervously at her twin, who turned his mouth down in a grimace.

"I mean that my people designed the catacombs," Gurthrunn replied. "Forget all the stories you ever heard about deadly dungeons and tombs constructed by evil wizards, demons and dark elves. They are *nothing* compared to us dwarves. Mark me well, children, Dweorgar have a true genius for such places. We will be lucky if all of us reach the treasure chamber. Perhaps none of us will."

"That's a cheery thought, how very encouraging!" Not bothering to hide his sarcasm, Lar scowled at Gurthrunn, who shrugged.

"But we have you and that map," Anna said. "That must count for something."

"I have never been here before, and this map is probably

out of date. In any event I doubt it will help much. My people do not leave plans showing the traps and pitfalls and denizens."

"Traps?" asked Wilburh.

"Pitfalls?" asked Ellette

"Denizens?" asked Hild. "What are they?"

"I think he means the creatures that live there," said Wilburh.

"Indeed," the dwarf answered. Pushing his war hammer into his belt, he reached up with his arms, one hand grasping each of the huge brass door rings. He glanced back at them all.

"Well then, children, shall we go in?"

# CHAPTER NINE

## CATACOMBS

Gurthrunn heaved on the rings, and with a loud creak the huge doors slid slowly open. As they peered inside, the children saw a wide stone passageway that stretched away from them down into the hillside. Mounted on the walls at either side were sconces in which torches flickered wildly in the sudden draught from the now open doorway. At the far end, about fifty paces away, was another set of double doors. The floor was lined with stone slabs, but just inside the entrance, in a wide strip some twelve feet long, a section of the floor was painted silver, its surface decorated with runic letters written in gold.

Wilburh squinted at the letters. They were similar to the runic script in which the village scrolls were written, but he did not recognise any of the words.

Gurthrunn saw him looking, and grunted, "You won't have seen them before. They are Dweorgish words, similar to the Vanir written language, which is the oldest script in the universe and the source of all magic."

"What do they say?" Anna asked.

"*Let none but those with the heart of a Dweorgar pass,*" Gurthrunn translated.

"What happens if someone without the heart of a Dweorgar enters?" Hild asked in a small voice.

"They are destroyed," he replied, and then turned back to Kendra, who along with the Svartálfar was watching from a few yards away.

"Let me do this alone," he called out. "I need not endanger the children. We cannot be sure about this barrier or know if it will let them pass."

"What is the problem, Dweorgar? Are you afraid for your little pets?" the Svartálfar captain taunted, waving one of the dark elves forward. It ran to do the captain's bidding and poked a spear at Anna. Gurthrunn simply reached

over, seized the creature by its throat and tossed it over his shoulder through the doorway. The dark elf screeched in terror as it tumbled through the air. As it passed above the silver strip, the elf glowed brighter and brighter, and then with a final scream it disintegrated into ash, which now wafted downwards in the breeze.

"Merciful Woden," Lar gasped. "So that's what happens!"

The dwarf turned back to the Valkyrie. "I will not ask them to take this risk, Kendra."

"The agreement is that you all enter, Dweorgar. I am sure they will be safe," she replied.

"But none of us has the heart of a Dweorgar," Anna protested, staring in horror at Kendra, who ignored her.

Gurthrunn shrugged. "The Valkyrie believes that it all comes down to what the Dweorgar language here says and what it actually means."

"I don't understand," Ellette said, and from the blank faces of Lar, Anna and Hild it was clear they were just as confused.

Not so Wilburh, however. "It's like a riddle," he said, "the sort Raedann might ask of an evening in the mead hall when he tries to trick us by making us guess the wrong thing. Once you find the answer it's all very obvious really. The phrase might say 'The heart of a Dweorgar', but actually mean something else."

Hild frowned. "Like what?"

"Think about it," said her twin. "What makes the Dweorgar different from the Vanir, the Æsir and the other immortal creatures like elves and Valkyries?"

The other children looked mystified and did not answer.

"They are mortal and have souls," Wilburh explained. "So you see then that this phrase, 'The heart of a Dweorgar', might actually mean their *soul*. We are mortal too. We are human and we each have a soul. Therefore the barrier should let us pass," he finished.

"Your boy is clever, dwarf," Kendra said. "Let him go first."

"No!" Gurthrunn exclaimed. "We cannot be certain he is right. My people may have meant literally that only a Dweorgar can enter."

"Find out now!" Kendra snapped. She clicked her fingers at the Svartálfar, who shuffled forward, spears and scimitars at the ready.

Anna drew her sword, and within a heartbeat Gurthrunn's war hammer was in his hand.

"Stop, we cannot fight them all!" Wilburh exclaimed. Then suddenly, before he had time to think about what he was doing, he stepped over the threshold and onto the silver strip…

And he was still alive! He took four more steps, then stood beyond it in the passageway.

"Er…hello?" he called.

Eyes wide, the others turned and stared at him.

There was a moment of shocked surprise before Kendra spoke. "Well now, clever *and* brave it seems – or perhaps foolish. Whichever, it now appears to answer your questions. I suggest you get on with it."

"Oh, very well. Come on, children, follow me. The doorway is safe it seems," Gurthrunn said, hurrying across the shining strip to join Wilburh in the passageway.

"It's those traps, pitfalls and denizens that worry me," Lar said to no one in particular as he too stepped over the threshold. Anna went next, then Ellette, and last of all Hild, who kept her eyes tightly shut as she followed them over.

Watching from the passageway, Wilburh saw that

Kendra had moved forward and now stood in the doorway. He prayed that she would keep coming, or trip and fall onto the silver strip, but she was too clever for that.

"You have one day, Dweorgar," she shouted, her words echoing in the passageway. "Just one day to find the items I need." She pointed up at the sky. "See how the sun is at its zenith even now? Mark my words, if you have not returned with the items I need by the time the sun is once again high overhead, then the bard you call Raedann will die." With those words she pushed the doors to, slamming them shut and sealing the companions inside the catacombs.

Gurthrunn reached up and pulled a flaming torch out of a wall sconce. "Come on," he said, heading for the interior doors which were identical to the ones they had just passed through. When they reached them, the dwarf listened for a second and then waved Ellette forward. "Your ears are sharpest, can you hear anything within this portal?"

Ellette scuttled up to stand beside the dwarf and bent her ear to the door. After a moment she shook her head. "No, I can't hear anything." Gurthrunn nodded his thanks and then heaved open the two doors. A gust of cold, slightly stale air rushed into the children's faces, making Ellette blink.

Beyond them was a chamber about the size of Nerian's hall back in Scenestane, though unlike the Headman's hall, this room was not built of wood and thatch. The walls were hewn from stone; the ceiling, also stone, was supported by six stone pillars, and the floor was lined with great stone slabs. Like the passageway behind them, it was illuminated by torches, but these were mounted on the pillars, as well as above the four doors that led out of the room. There was one door on each wall. Through one of these they had, of course, just entered. Two of the other three were smaller single doors, both made of sturdy oak and reinforced by bars and studs of iron. The third, a large, heavy iron door, was in the opposite wall to where the companions now gathered, peering into the chamber which, apart from a long oak table in the centre and half a dozen matching chairs, appeared to be empty.

They all moved into the room and Lar shut the double doors behind them.

"Why is that middle door made of iron?" Ellette said, taking a few steps towards it. "Makes you wonder what is behind it."

"Wait. Stop, Ellette, everyone, I need to tell you something," Wilburh said. "It's about what happened in the library room just now."

They all stared at him. "Well, go on, tell us," said Ellette, backing away from the iron door and swinging round to face him.

Taking a deep breath, Wilburh described hearing the voice of Ullr inside his head and what the god had told him. The children gaped at him, eyebrows raised, clearly wondering if he was going mad, but Gurthrunn seemed to accept what he said without question.

"Ullr definitely said Gambantein?" he asked when Wilburh had finished.

Wilburh nodded. "That's what it sounded like."

"And he said it was here in the catacombs?"

"Yes, and he said we needed to take it. At least, I assume that is what he meant, but he was more than half asleep." Wilburh frowned. "He was going to say more, I'm sure of it, but Kendra was moving towards me so I had to pretend I was just feeling dizzy, and then all my hearing came back and I saw that Ullr's eyes had closed..."

"What is this Gambantein and why is it so important?" Lar asked Gurthrunn.

"It is a sword – a powerful blade, yet it is a cursed, dark weapon. I am not sure why it is so important to Ullr. I wonder why he wants us to take it."

"It might be something to do with Gleipnir," Wilburh said, trying to remember the god's exact words.

"You may be right." The dwarf frowned.

"So, we know what we need to find, both for Kendra and for Ullr," said Lar. "What we don't know is which way to go," he pondered, pointing at the various doors.

"Does the map help?" Hild asked.

Gurthrunn pulled out the roll of parchment and spread it out on the table, weighing down one end with his war hammer and the other with his knife. The children crowded round.

"Alright then, here is the entranceway, so this must be the chamber we are now in. Look, see it does have three exits." Gurthrunn gestured first at a long passageway and then at the rectangle that connected to it.

Lar tapped his index finger on the map. "According to this the middle doorway, the one opposite the entrance, leads more directly to the treasure chamber. The other two lead into a maze of passageways. It seems pretty straightforward to me. I thought you said your people were clever with these things. Don't we just go straight on?"

Gurthrunn shook his head. "I very much doubt it," he sighed, "but I suppose we must check it out. Ellette, go and listen at the other two doors and have a peep round them if you can. Lar and Anna, you had best go with her in case there is anything in the rooms beyond."

"*Anything*?" Lar asked. He rolled his eyes. "Oh, I see – denizens!"

"Exactly," Gurthrunn grunted, rolling up the map and handing it to Wilburh as the three pattered over to the right-hand door. Ellette bent to listen. After a moment she reached up and gently turned the handle. The door opened a few inches, and she peered inside then closed it again.

"The room beyond is similar to this one with a door in each wall. It appears to be empty," she said, walking to the other door, Anna and Lar on her heels. Repeating the process with the left-hand door, she turned back to Gurthrunn. "This room is a mirror to the other. It is also empty."

"Very well," he said, "try the iron door opposite, but be cautious, Ellette. There will be a reason it is different from the others."

She nodded and turned towards it, followed closely by her escort. As she did so, Wilburh leant closer to Gurthrunn so that Hild, standing nearby, would not hear him.

"Ullr told me he could only speak to me because I have great mystical powers," he murmured.

"I would agree," grunted the dwarf.

"Why then have I been unable to do magic this last day or so?"

"I had noticed your difficulty earlier." Gurthrunn studied him. "I assumed you were just tired, maybe."

Wilburh shook his head. "No, I don't think that's it – so why is it happening?"

The Dweorgar opened his mouth to answer, but before he could do so there was a huge roar of rage from the room beyond the iron door. Ellette squealed in surprise and tumbled out of the way as the door swung open.

They all turned to stare in horror as an eruption of flame billowed out of the opening, missing Ellette by mere inches.

# CHAPTER TEN

## WILBURH'S PROBLEM

They stared at the open doorway in growing trepidation as the burst of fire receded. After a moment the glow from beyond the portal increased again, and soon a deep red light was radiating through it. It was accompanied by a crackling and popping and a low roaring sound. Air seemed to be sucked out of their room and towards the door, and a draught as powerful as a strong gale tugged and pulled at them all. Resisting it, they backed away, Ellette having scrambled onto her feet.

The temperature in the outer room where they stood suddenly increased. To Wilburh it felt as if they were standing near one of the bread ovens in Scenestane when someone had just opened the door. Indeed, it was hotter even than that. Almost, in fact, as if they were standing too close to the bonfire on Midsummer's Day. He shuddered, feeling something approaching the door; something huge and powerful; something terrifying.

And then…it appeared.

The entity that now came into view was like a whirlwind – except it was composed entirely of flame and fire rather than air. This, though, was fire that swirled and spun as it moved. It was a maelstrom of heat: an inferno. Arm-like protrusions bulged out of it, and then retreated back into it again to emerge moments later on a different side. Towards the top of the whirlwind two eye-shaped ovals of a deeper red regarded them with malevolence.

"It's a fire spirit!" Lar shouted and let fly with an arrow. It struck the fire creature, but at once ignited and burnt to ash in a heartbeat without having any noticeable effect. Raising her shield, Anna stepped forward and swung at the being with her sword. This dug deep into its side and the resultant roar of pain suggested it had at least caused some injury, but when Anna withdrew the sword the wound instantly filled with fire, and after a moment there was no sign of any damage.

The fire elemental erupted into the room in a wave of heat and fury. It smashed into Anna's shield, sending her spinning backwards and tumbling head over heels while it rushed on by her. Then it hesitated a moment, rotating slowly on the spot, apparently examining them each in turn. In the few moments' respite, Ellette slotted a pebble in her sling, spun it round her head and let fly. The pebble bounced off the elemental's fiery surface, the only apparent effect being to draw the fire spirit's attention to Ellette, who squealed as it now surged roaring towards her.

Wilburh thought quickly. Clutching his rune sticks he focused upon them, summoning their strength and using them to direct the spell he now cast. Shouting *"Egorstréamas!"* he thrust his arms out, his hands held open towards the flames.

He had expected a torrent of water to come flooding out of his fingers, and yet the result was nowhere near so impressive. Instead, a fairly pathetic spray of raindrops flew forth from his hands and impacted on the flank of the flame creature. When the water droplets made contact with the fire they sizzled, turned instantly to steam and were gone. Yet despite the disappointing result, the fire spirit once again roared as if in pain and, spinning away from Ellette, it came for Wilburh.

He recoiled in horror and then dropped into a crouch, arms wrapping around his head as the fire beast surged towards him.

"*Nidarvellir*!" bellowed Gurthrunn and, leaping past Wilburh, he charged directly at the flaming creature.

Holding his shield in front of him, his war hammer clutched in his right hand, the dwarf slammed his weapon into the beast with all his force. Still bellowing his war cry he pushed the creature backwards and away from Wilburh.

By now Anna had clambered to her feet. Following Gurthrunn's example, she ran to his side and rammed her shield into the elemental. Fire lapped around the edges and scorched the skin on her arms, but Anna, groaning with pain, held on tight to her shield. Slowly, side by side, she and the chain-clad dwarf pushed the creature back towards the middle doorway. Reaching it, both of them red-faced and sweating heavily from heat and exertion, they gave one final push, but the fire spirit flung out two arms of flame and latched onto the door frame, bracing itself in the opening.

Dropping his bow, Lar leapt across to the doorway and, drawing his seax, began to hack and cut at the elemental's nearest arm. The steel blade dug deep and the creature screamed, letting go of the door frame. With a final almighty effort, the dwarf and Anna shoved the fire spirit back over the threshold. Ellette was there ready, clutching the iron door handle and grimacing as the heat of it burnt her fingers.

"NOW!" shouted Gurthrunn.

As he and Anna leapt out of the way, Ellette slammed the door shut and Lar slipped the bar into place. There were two huge bangs as the creature rammed into the other side, but the door was sturdy and it held. Then, with a final roar of frustration, the elemental being was gone.

"Well," Ellette said, shaking her hand and panting to catch her breath, "now we know what's behind the iron door!"

There was a moment's silence as they all stared at her and then at each other, and then Lar said dryly, "I assume that was one of the denizens."

"Yes," said Gurthrunn, "that's exactly what it was."

"I guess we are not going that way then."

The dwarf shook his head. "We cannot easily fight that. We will have to take the long way round, I think."

"What *was* that thing?" Ellette asked.

"Remember the ice elementals from Niflheim? This is their opposite: a fire elemental from Muspelheim, the world of fire. My people must have trapped one and brought it here to help them guard the treasures."

At that moment Anna gave a gasp of pain and, holding her arm, slumped down into a crouch. Hild rushed over and, taking hold of Anna's hand, examined her arm. "These are nasty burns, Anna. I must apply a marigold and beewort poultice. Luckily I carry all the ingredients," she said, patting the large medicine pouch at her waist. "It will take a little while to prepare. Ellette, I think you should let me dress your hand too. What about you, Lar? Gurthrunn? Are either of you hurt?"

The dwarf shook his head. "My Dweorgar skin is a lot tougher than your human skin, but thank you, Hild."

She nodded, led Anna to the table and had her sit on one of the chairs while she rummaged in her pack and pouches, pulling out various items and herbs. She was soon busily preparing a salve.

While Hild was occupied, Gurthrunn turned to Wilburh. The boy was still crouching down, cradling the rune sticks. When he saw the dwarf looking at him, he shook his head.

"I don't think I can manage this task – as you saw, my effort was pathetic. I can't handle even basic magic now."

"You will be able to, lad. I have confidence that you will regain the power before the end," Gurthrunn said.

"How though? It's all very well having confidence, but it is I who must make it happen, and the power has deserted me."

"Maybe you are not doing the spells right..." Ellette suggested.

"Of course I am doing them right, silly girl."

"I only asked," she said, hurt.

"Well don't!" he snapped. "Oh, just leave me alone, all of you." Scowling, he stomped over to the corner of the room and turned his back to them all. He knew he was being foolish and that it was not anyone else's fault. He had not meant to shout at Ellette, but he was frustrated, scared even, and that had made him lash out.

There was a moment's awkward silence, then Anna asked Gurthrunn a question. Her voice suggested she was just asking it to fill the uncomfortable pause. Yet it was a good question, and despite knowing some of the facts himself, Wilburh turned to listen to the answer.

"Can you tell us about Gleipnir and why it is so strong that even gods are powerless against it?"

Gurthrunn nodded. "The gods are all powerful, but as we know, the God Loki is treacherous. He was always acting against the others, whether in the open or in secret. It is said that he created one of the greatest of all beasts, intending that it should devour the other gods, leaving him supreme. When he released it, the gods tried to capture the creature, hoping to kill it, but so powerful was it that they failed."

The children listened carefully. They had already heard Raedann's tale of the wolf, Fenrir, but never before had it seemed quite as important to them as it did now.

"The gods attempted to bind Fenrir with huge chains of metal, but the wolf was able to break out of these with ease. So they commissioned my people – the dwarves – to forge a chain that was impossible to break. The greatest forgers and artificers of my race were baffled as to how they could achieve this seemingly impossible task. It was my own forefather who suggested that the only way to fashion such a chain was to create it out of six impossible things." Gurthrunn held up his hands, and on his fingers counted out the list that followed.

"First the sound of a cat's footfall, second the beard of a woman, third the roots of a mountain, fourth the sinews of a bear, fifth the breath of a fish and sixth the spittle of a bird. How they collected these items and how they brought them together is a secret known only to a few, but in the end, even though Gleipnir is as thin as a silken ribbon, it is stronger than iron or steel, or indeed any metal. Many other enchantments were placed upon it so that it would subdue and tap the strength of any entity it bound. That is why it is so strong, and why even the Vanir gods now lie dormant."

"Along with poor old Raedann," Hild said, looking up for a moment from where she was busily pounding dried marigold petals and beewort ready to mix with rosemary oil, which she carried in a small, dark bottle in her pack along with the miniature pestle and mortar and a variety of other medicaments and bandages.

"Then how can we free them?" Ellette asked.

"That I do not know," Gurthrunn answered. He was silent for a while, distractedly watching as Hild deftly smeared the salve she had made onto Anna's burns.

"There you are, that should stop them blistering and will ease the pain." She smiled at her friend.

"Thanks, Hild, that's really soothing."

Hild turned her attention to Ellette and then Lar, who had meantime retrieved his bow and slung it on his back. Neither was as severely burnt as Anna, who now stood, picked up her sword and shield and looked at Gurthrunn, a question in her eyes.

He nodded. "I think we should carry on. That is if you

have finished sulking," he said, turning to Hild's twin.

Wilburh felt his face go scarlet. "I'm sorry...I am just... just confused."

"We will sort it out, Wilburh. Don't be upset," Anna said, laying a sympathetic hand on his shoulder.

Easy for you to say, he thought to himself, but did not say it, for she was trying to be kind. He just nodded and replied, "Let's go on."

While he was waiting for Hild to repack her things, Gurthrunn examined the three doors for a moment. "Well then, we cannot go straight on, so we must decide to go left or right. How shall we choose?"

They all thought about this for a moment, and then Lar shrugged and, reaching into his belt pouch, pulled out an old Roman coin.

"Let's flip for it," he said.

# Chapter Eleven

## Wheels and Blades

The coin landed on the table, revealing the head of some long dead Roman emperor. This meant they had chosen the left-hand door. Ellette carefully opened it and slipped into the room. The others followed her, closing the door behind them. They found that in this chamber there were again three potential exits – another three doors, one in each of the other walls. Ellette cautiously examined them in turn, bending to press her ear against each door to listen. Returning to the middle of the room where the others were gathered, she reported back to them.

"I can't hear anything beyond any of the doors. Which way do we go?"

Retrieving the map from Wilburh, Lar looked down at it then pointed at the right-hand door. "That one leads on into the complex and is the shorter route."

"Shorter routes are not always the best. What if there is another of those fire spirits in there?" Hild pointed out with a tremble in her voice.

"We can't plan on what might be, lass, only on what is," Gurthrunn suggested.

"I agree," said Anna. "Let us take the shortest route unless we have good reason to do otherwise."

Wilburh and Ellette both nodded in agreement. The

small girl scuttled over to the chosen exit, listened carefully again and then tried the door. It opened. She gently pushed it a few inches and peered within.

"Merciful Woden!" she exclaimed. "I think you had all better come and look."

They did. The room beyond the door was a narrow chamber, perhaps sixty paces long and twenty wide. On either side of the room huge stone wheels protruded from the walls; at present about half of each one was visible. Each wheel bore viciously sharp blades that projected from the rims by about six inches. The ground in front of the wheels bore a groove cut deep into the stone of the chamber floor. It seemed obvious that the wheels were designed to roll forward along these grooves. The wheels on the left-hand wall were slightly offset compared with those on the right, so that if the wheels rolled forward they would interlock like the fingers of a man's hands: two huge stone hands coming together to slice and crush whatever lay between them.

"What sets them off, do you think?" Hild asked, peering between the shoulders of Gurthrunn and Lar.

"Let's find out," Ellette chirped, and without warning stepped into the room. The moment she did so there was a deep grinding noise from the floor beneath her feet followed by a mechanical clunk-clunk sound. An instant later the wheels sprang into motion.

Not a moment too soon, Ellette jumped back. The speed with which the wheels whirled forwards was breathtakingly quick, the blades becoming a blur. They rolled down the full length of the groove, paused briefly, and then spun back into the wall before beginning another cycle. They each moved out at a slightly different moment, so that at any time some were still embedded in the walls while others were half way along the grooves and others all the way out.

"That's impossible. No one can get past this," Anna said.

"How on earth do your people get through this maze if things like that creature or traps like this confront them at every turn?" Hild asked.

Gurthrunn glanced at her. "There will be a key or lever, or maybe a switch in the room that will deactivate the device. However, it will not be at this end. The idea would be that the guardians activate the traps as they pass through them deeper into the labyrinth," he said.

"That's great. The switch to stop the trap is beyond the trap. That doesn't exactly help us, does it," Lar said irritably. "How are we supposed to get through?"

"We are not. That's the whole point, Child of Midgard!" Gurthrunn replied, his tone ominous.

"Well we obviously can't go this way, can we," Anna said. "Let's try the other doors."

They moved across to the door that lay opposite the entrance and Ellette tried it. It was locked.

"Give me a moment," the little girl said and fumbled in her pack. After a while spent sorting through her belongings, she produced a collection of bronze tools. There was a set of tweezers and a couple of small picks like the blunt needles they all used to clean dirt from under their fingernails. Crouching down in front of the door, she slid one into the lock and then fiddled with it, her tongue sticking out as she concentrated.

"A-ha!" she exclaimed in joy as there was a click and the door popped open a couple of inches.

"I didn't know you could do that," Lar said, his voice filled with admiration. Then he frowned. "Hey! I just thought. Last week I got blamed for stealing the salted pork from the food store, despite it being locked and bolted. Father said it was me and clouted me for it, but it wasn't me, it was you, wasn't it! *You* pinched it, didn't you, Little Elf."

Ellette blushed. "Sorry, but it was very nice pork," she answered with a smile and, turning back, pulled open the door. Then her smile vanished as beyond the doorway she spotted not another room, but a solid wall. The door led nowhere.

"Woden's earwax!" she cursed as she climbed back onto her feet and stared at the wall.

"Try the third door," Anna suggested wearily. They all plodded over to the final door. Ellette listened again, but not hearing anything, tried the handle. This door was unlocked and swung open easily revealing a small chamber beyond, about the size of the food lockup at Scenestane. This room was apparently empty, apart from a small glass sphere lying on the ground in the exact centre of the floor.

They all eyed the sphere, noticing that inside it was a swirling vapour that looked like a blue mist. "I don't get it, what's that?" Lar asked, peering at the globe. "Let me take a look." He stepped into the room.

"No! Wait, don't do that!" Ellette shouted, but she was too late.

The moment Lar set foot inside the door there was a loud bang and the sphere shattered, scattering shards of glass, and a cloud of blue smoke erupted outwards.

"Close the door!" Anna shouted as Lar backed frantically out of the room.

Ellette heaved on the door, but it would not budge. "It's stuck!" she cried.

The smoke was now wafting into the outer chamber where they stood. Wilburh breathed some in. He felt an immediate burning in his throat and lungs and started coughing violently.

"Poison...it's poisoned," he croaked.

"Come away!" Gurthrunn shouted. "Back into the outer chamber everyone!"

They rushed to open the door into the room with the table, but when Lar reached it and yanked on the handle, he found it too was stuck. The poisonous gas cloud was pouring out into the room now and they were all beginning to cough.

"Let me try," Gurthrunn said, putting all of his immense strength into his attempts to heave on the handle. It was no good, it was not moving. Backing away, he shook his head. "It's hopeless," he rasped. "There is some kind of deadlock in use. It must be set to trigger when the sphere shatters. I doubt we could even smash it down. We will have to risk the blades and wheels!" He led the way back to the first room they had tried.

They found that the door to this room had popped open, and it also was now immobile. Ellette, Gurthrunn and Lar entered, and as they did so the wheel trap mechanism sprang into life once more, the spinning wheels of stone and whirling blades of steel threatening to slash or crush anyone foolhardy enough to try the passage between them.

Lar shook his head. "We can't. It's madness. No one can get past them."

Coughing and spluttering, eyes streaming, they stared at the contraption in dismay.

"The gas has reached us," Hild gasped, holding her hand over her mouth and nose.

Wilburh, standing next to her, sighed and, holding his rune sticks out in front of him, tried a spell. "*Windræs*" he said, directing his hands towards the blue cloud. A slight breeze sprang up, fighting against the gas and holding it back. "Not as powerful as I'd hoped. I'm afraid it will not hold it back for long," he muttered.

Only Hild replied. Reaching out a sympathetic hand, she patted his shoulder. "But it's holding it back for now, that's better than nothing."

"Not a lot," said Lar.

"So what do we do?" Anna said. "We can't stay here, we'll be gassed to death. I'm willing to give the wheels a try, but I don't think I'd get through those blades."

"But I would," Ellette replied. "I am the smallest and fastest. I can beat them."

"Are you sure, Daughter of Midgard?" Gurthrunn peered at her from beneath his bushy eyebrows.

"That's madness. We can't let you go, Little Elf," Lar said, sounding very protective.

"Oh let me try." She grinned at him. "There's a slim chance I'll get through. It's either death from this gas or from those blades."

Gurthrunn shrugged. "She is right, Lar."

Lar looked about to argue, but a fresh bout of coughing from Hild interrupted him. Slowly he nodded. "Oh, go on then," he said, holding out his hand. "Here, Little Elf, give me your pack, but if you die I will be very cross indeed!"

"I'm touched," she joked, shrugging out of her pack and tossing it to him then flashing him a cheeky smile as she moved forward.

The wheels were spinning back and forth, interlocking and moving apart. The slight delay between one pair of wheels and the next set meant that there was a ripple of movement, rather like a wave moving along a beach.

Ellette studied the movement, counting softly, getting an idea of the rhythm and pace of the device. Meanwhile, Wilburh was chanting away with his spell, desperately trying to hold the gas back. He started coughing as he inhaled another lungful and that interrupted his spell. The impediment lifted, the gas surged forward, forcing Hild and Wilburh to back away further – right into Lar.

"Careful, you almost knocked me onto the wheels!" he snapped.

"Sorry, but..." Wilburh gasped then coughed "...the gas is here."

Ellette glanced at them, grimacing as she too noticed the gas infiltrating the wheel room. It was now or never, and she knew it. A determined expression came to her face and her body tensed. There was a pause, and then she was off.

She had timed her start so that she reached the first pair of overlapping wheels just as they were moving apart. She dashed into the gap between them, a mere hair's breadth

from the vicious blade points on either side.

On she sped, reaching each pair of wheels just as they were parting. She was doing well, but as she ran she sped up with each step, and that was the cause of the trouble on the last pair of wheels. She reached them a fraction too early, just as the wheels had arrived at the midpoint and the way ahead was blocked.

Trying to slow down, Ellette realised that she could not do so in time. Instead she leapt high, tumbling forwards right over the spinning wheels. Her reactions were fast, but her legs were short, and despite the mighty leap she could not quite clear the blade points, which slashed and cut at her chest and belly. As the points dug deep, she let out a scream and fell to the ground just beyond the wheels – a crumpled, bloody figure.

"Ellette!" shouted Lar in alarm, stepping forward to try to move towards her and then stepping back from the whirling blades.

"I...I am alive," Ellette answered, lifting her head, "but it hurts. I think I have been cut about ten times."

"Ellette, you were superb, but now if you possibly can, you must look for the switch," Anna said, coughing. "We cannot survive this gas much longer."

"Must I?" Ellette sounded faint, her voice feeble.

"Yes, Daughter of Midgard," Gurthrunn answered. "Hild will heal you, but we can't get to you."

"Alright...I'll try. What am I looking for?"

"Brave lass," the dwarf said. "Look around the doorway. There might be a button or lever or even a panel you can push in."

Ellette dragged herself to her feet, her hands clutching her stomach. They could all see blood dripping from several wounds as she stumbled over to the doorway and looked around. She searched for what seemed like an age. Then suddenly her hand darted forwards and she pressed a part of the wall. From where the children and Gurthrunn were standing it seemed no different from the rest, yet it clearly was, because a few moments after she had pressed it there was a clunking sound from deep in the floor beneath their feet, and then the wheels slid back into the walls and stopped turning. Ellette had found the switch.

They all dashed forward to where the little girl had slumped to the ground.

"You did well, Little Elf," said Lar. "Very well…that was as brave as anything I've seen."

She gave a thin smile. "If only I was not so little I might have made that last jump."

Gently lifting Ellette's dress to examine her wounds, Hild nodded. "It's not as bad as it looks," she murmured, searching in her pack and lifting out a sharp bone needle, some thread, jars of salve and strips of cloth. "There's just one cut that needs stitching and binding, the others are not too deep. Lay still, Ellette, and chew on this." She put something black on the little girl's tongue. "It's just willow bark. It will help take away the pain."

The others left her to it and pulled away. "You dwarves are twisted individuals if you ask me," Lar said to Gurthrunn, a bitter edge to his voice as he heard Ellette whimpering.

"I did say this would be dangerous. I told you that we Dweorgar are experts at this kind of thing. And much as I wish right now that it were not so, these traps were put here for a very good reason: to stop powerful artefacts getting into the wrong hands."

"Hands like Kendra's," Lar said angrily.

"Hands like Kendra's," the dwarf gloomily agreed.

They sat down against the wall and rested while Hild

worked. After a time Anna asked Gurthrunn a question. "Why do you think Ullr wants Gambantein?"

"It is a powerful weapon, not just a sharp blade, although it is certainly that, but it can burst into flame or shine like the sun. It once belonged to the Vanir God, Frey, until he gave it away. He now lives in Asgard."

"Gave it away to whom?" Anna asked.

"Well, according to the legends Frey fell deeply in love with a beautiful giantess called Gerdr, but she would not marry him. However, Frey's persuasive servant eventually got her to agree to the marriage and Frey was so grateful he gave Gambantein to the servant as a reward. Frey's Vanir kin did not approve of the marriage, nor did the Æsir. Certainly none of them approved of his giving away such a powerful weapon to a servant. Nevertheless, this is what occurred. No one knows what happened to it then. I can only surmise that the Vanir gods got their hands on it, hid it away in these catacombs and said nothing about it. I've no idea what became of the servant, but..."

"What can it do, this sword?" Lar interrupted. "Apart from burst into flame, that is."

"It was a Vanir blade and may have been created to serve in the wars between the Vanir and the Æsir when, eons ago, the two races of the gods fought each other. Eventually they made peace and exchanged hostages – that is how Frey and his sister Freya came to live in Asgard. The gods are now at peace and have been for a very long time, but the blade was made by the Vanir in the days when this was not so. So it is a sword that can defeat the Æsir and anything they cause to be made."

"Like Gleipnir?" Anna suggested.

Gurthrunn stared at her. "You are wise for your young years, shield maiden. Gambantein might be the only object that could sever the golden thread."

"I think that must be what Ullr was trying to tell me when he was overcome by sleep," Wilburh said.

Lar whistled. "Well then, we have a reason for why Ullr needs it. If we can get the sword to the library we can use it to free the Vanir gods."

"If we can find it and persuade the guardians to part with it, that is!" Anna said.

"Well yes," Lar replied, "there is that!"

"And if we can get it to the library without being stopped by the troll, the Svartálfar and Kendra," Anna added.

"Yes, that too," Lar said.

"Easy job then," Wilburh mumbled.

Over near the door Ellette was climbing to her feet. Hild had finished her work and the little girl looked less pale than she had done a few moments before.

"You alright, Little Elf?" asked Lar, frowning with anxiety at the bulge of bandaging that was visible under her dress.

"I feel like a sieve and I'm sore, but thanks to Hild and her willow bark I'm not in too much pain. I'll manage well enough." She stared down at them all sitting against the wall. "Well then," she said, tapping her foot with impatience, "what are we waiting for? Let's get on with it."

Laughing with relief, Lar jumped to his feet. "Yes, let's."

# Chapter Twelve

## The Power Within

The door that Ellette had gone to such pains to reach was in fact unlocked. It led into a long corridor, lit by torches burning in three iron sconces evenly positioned along its length. The injured girl took the lead as they proceeded down it, Lar insisting that he continue to carry her pack. The flickering flames made their shadows almost skip and dance along the wall to their right. They walked in silence, making the sound of their footsteps echoing down the chamber seem loud. Finally they reached the far end where another door barred further progress. This one was locked, and so they paused while Ellette, still protesting that she could manage, knelt and got to work with her set of tools.

Once unlocked, the door opened out into a large pillared hall that stretched away to their right and appeared to be empty. There were three doors on each of the long sides of this hall, including the door through which they had just entered. The six companions halted to peer down the length of the hall, fearful of finding another trap. Nothing happened. After a moment, escorted by a vigilant Lar and Anna, Ellette set off to investigate each door in turn. Hild, Wilburh and Gurthrunn held back and watched them.

While they waited, Wilburh once again took the opportunity to pose the question uppermost in his mind.

"Gurthrunn," he said softly, "why...why do you think I can't do magic anymore?"

The dwarf studied him for a long time without answering. Then he scratched his beard and said, "How did you learn to do magic in the first place? Who taught you?"

Wilburh frowned. "No one taught me as such. I guess I have always been curious about the stories of the gods, and one day, when I was about five or six, I saw Iden, our priest, looking at the scrolls he keeps hidden in the temple. Somehow they seemed wondrous to me, and I sneaked back into the temple, found the scrolls and tried to understand them. When I unrolled them I discovered they were covered in runes, although some also showed pictures. The pictures helped me get some idea of what was written, but I knew that the words themselves held the real story...the real power. I got frustrated and shouted out, 'Oh, I wish I could read.' That was when Iden walked in. I thought he would be angry, and so he was a little at first, but he had heard what I had said, and a few days later he talked to my mother and asked her to let me study as an acolyte. She was doubtful at first, but in the end she agreed, so Iden taught me to read and he let me study his holy scrolls. I learnt a lot about the gods through those scrolls. I found out how the Æsir gods, and in particular Woden, learnt magic from the Vanir, and about rune sticks and their use in casting spells."

Rummaging in his pouch, Wilburh retrieved the rune sticks and examined them, cradling them in his hands. "Iden gave me these to study. He explained that each was engraved with several runes that combined to call upon the power of certain gods. That power was embedded in the sticks, and so was there for anyone to use who had the ability. In fact I don't think Iden himself can do much magic beyond a little healing, and I don't think he suspected that I would be able to do any either. Yet I studied the scrolls and soon discovered the words that triggered the spells. The spells needed power though, and I didn't seem to have enough to make them work. Then one day, when I was holding them, I focused on the sticks, said the words and accidentally set fire to one of the tapestries on the temple wall. After I had put the fire out I realised what had happened. I had drawn upon the power in the sticks, and that is what made the spells work..."

Wilburh halted because he had noticed that Gurthrunn was now frowning. Over on the far side of the pillared hall Ellette and Lar were peering around a door before closing it gently and moving on towards the next one.

"I think I see the problem, Wilburh," the dwarf said after a moment.

"What?"

"You believe, then, that the power you need to make the magic work comes from these sticks of wood?"

Wilburh nodded. "Doesn't it?"

Gurthrunn shrugged. "Iden is correct that there is power in the rune sticks, but he has the nature of it wrong. It is not just embedded once in the sticks by a priest summoning power from the gods. It is drawn into the sticks each and every time they are used. The sticks focus that power and direct it. What you are feeling in the sticks is leftover power, like the dregs at the bottom of a barrel of ale. That is your problem. You are tapping those dregs. At first, earlier in the summer, there was a lot of power left, and you used that power to good effect, as we all saw. Now, though, the barrel of ale is almost empty – the dregs of power all but gone."

"So that is why my spells are getting weaker?"

Gurthrunn nodded. "I believe so."

"So how do I get the power back into the sticks? How do I call upon the power of the gods?"

Gurthrunn now shook his head. "You misunderstand. For a priest the sticks channel power from the gods in small amounts. But a sorcerer does not channel from the gods. He or she has the power within himself or herself. In the case of a sorcerer, the rune sticks' purpose is to focus the power of the wielder. The sticks can help you, but first you must learn to find your own power: the power within yourself."

Now it was Wilburh who was frowning. "My own power? What power?"

"Well, that is the point. You were never taught this by a sorcerer, you learnt it yourself under the uncertain guidance of a priest who had little power himself and did not know how to teach you. So you learnt the spells, but not how to channel your power into them. You improvised and

107

tapped the power in the rune sticks. But now that power is all but gone, which leaves us with one very important question."

"Which is?"

"Are you a sorcerer? Do you *have* any real power yourself, or is it all borrowed power? If it is your own, can you learn how to focus it and use it to drive the spells?"

Hild, who had been watching Ellette and the others, now turned to look at her twin. Transferring her gaze to Gurthrunn, she said with a smile, "I am sure he can."

"I hope so. But I cannot help you, lad. You have to learn this yourself."

"He will. He is very clever," Hild said.

Wilburh smiled thinly at her. *What if she is wrong? he asked himself. What if everything I did was through borrowed power, like Gurthrunn said? If I am a fraud then this whole journey – coming here to gain a spell from the Vanir gods – is just a waste of time. If I have no power the village will be in danger and I will be able to do nothing to defeat Kendra.*

As he pondered on these glum thoughts, Ellette, Anna and Lar returned from their reconnaissance.

"Well, what did you find?" Gurthrunn asked.

"Of the two other doors on this side of the hall, we are convinced the middle one leads back into the fire elemental's room. We think the third will just take us back down to the entrance chamber," Anna said.

"What of the three on the opposite side? They must lead deeper into the catacombs."

"There appears to be a choice we must make," Ellette replied.

"Well of course..." Gurthrunn started to say, then frowned at her. "What exactly do you mean, child?"

"Well," said Lar before Ellette could answer, "how good are you dwarves at puzzles and riddles?" Then, gesturing with one hand, he led them on.

They all followed Lar and Ellette across the hall, weaving between the rows of pillars until they stood a little way in front of the middle door in the opposite wall.

"Each door is locked, and I could not hear anything beyond any of them," Ellette reported. "Having said that, the doors so far have been heavy and thick, so I don't think I trust my ears."

"What did you mean by 'puzzles and riddles'?" Wilburh asked Lar.

# CHAPTER THIRTEEN

## THREE WAYS

In answer, Lar moved to one side to reveal, set into the ground, a stone engraved with runes. "I could not read much of it," he said, "but there is an identical stone in front of the other two doors." He pointed first one way and then the other. "I did pick up a phrase about choosing a path, though."

"It's a pity none of you Angles of Mercia can read," Gurthrunn said grumpily to no-one in particular.

"Our priest can," protested Lar. "He taught Wilburh. And anyway, I can read a bit," he added defensively. "Raedann sometimes tells me what different runes mean when he is storytelling."

"Does he now," Gurthrunn grunted, moving forward to take a look at the script, but Wilburh got there first and, with a frown of concentration, bent over the stone, his finger moving along the runes as he read them under his breath, the dwarf craning over his shoulder.

ᚱᛖᛗ ᛏᚾᚱᛗᛗ ᚠᚠᛁᛃ ᛚᛕ ᛗᚠᛕ ᛚᚾᚠᚥᛃᛗ ᚠᛏᚺ ᚠᛁᛃᛗᚱᛚ ᛚᚾᚠᚥᛃᛗ ᛚᚠᛕ ᛗᛃᛃᛏ

ᛚᛏ ᚠᛁᛕᛗ ᚠ ᚠᚠᛕ ᛁᛁ ᛚᚾᚠᚥᛗᛏ ᛁᚠᛁᛗ ᚠᛏᚾᛗᚱ ᛗᚠᛕ ᛚᛕ ᛏᚠᛕ

ᛗ ᚺᚠ ᛁᚠᛏ ᚠᚥᚥᛗᚱ ᛚᛕ ᚠᛏ ᛗᚠᚥᛚ ᛚᚠᛏᚺ ᚠᚠᚱ ᛏᚺᚠᛏ ᛁᛁ ᛁᚠᛏ ᚠᛚᚱ ᛏᚠᚥᛚ

ᛁᚥᛁᛗᚠᚺ ᛏᚾᚱᛗᛗ ᚠᚠᛃ ᛏᚠ ᚺᛁᛗ ᚠᚱᛗ ᚠᛏᛏ ᚠᛗ ᚠᚥᚥᛗᚱ ᛏᚠ ᛚᛕ

"You were right, Lar, it does read very much like a riddle," Gurthrunn said.

"What does it say?" squeaked Ellette, hopping from one foot to the other.

"Like you said, that we've got a choice," said Wilburh. "Listen…"

Reading out loud, he translated the runes, occasionally corrected by Gurthrunn, for the language was archaic and the order of the words odd in places.

"*From three ways you may choose, and wisely choose you must.*

*But once a way is chosen none other may you take.*

*We do not offer you an easy path, for that is not our task.*

*Instead, three ways to die are all we offer to you.*

*Three chambers lie beyond these portals.*

*Water is the first challenge – the most treacherous of elements.*

*Air is the second – needed for life and much here we give thee.*

*A room beloved of birds.*

*The guardian of the third chamber requires a simple payment to pass.*

*Just that which thee must have that made it possible to enter.*

Which will you choose?"

As Wilburh's voice died away, they all looked at each other.

"Well," said Anna, "it seems clear enough that we have three doors, three chambers beyond and a choice of three challenges." She walked to the other two doors in that wall and peered down at each of the engraved stones. "How we tell which is which defeats me. The inscriptions all look identical."

"Maybe the left-hand door is the first chamber," Hild suggested.

"Why? It could just as easily be the right," Lar pointed out.

"What about the challenges then? What do we think they are?" Anna asked. "Is one easier than the others?"

Gurthrunn bit his lip as he pondered the question. "Probably not. My people were not making the route easy – they say as much in the engraving. Three potentially deadly challenges are what they offer."

"They like to tease, don't they," Lar observed, wandering over to lean against one of the pillars.

"It's not teasing, it's taunting," Gurthrunn corrected him with a shake of the head. "The former is gentle and harmless mayhap. The second is designed to hurt us. They want us to give up. They do not care whether it is sharp blades, fiery demons, gas-filled globes or our own minds that defeat us. So long as we turn back, they will have achieved their aim."

"Nasty people," Hild mumbled.

Gurthrunn shrugged. "Not really. Like I said, they are

protecting the treasury of the Vanir gods and with good reason. To them we are the enemy. Anyway, let us examine the choices: a room involving water. I am wearing full armour and will sink in that room. In addition I can't swim. So I am not keen. The second – the chamber of air – sounds safe enough, and yet we have that reference to it being beloved of birds. I think that means we would have to fly or something equally impossible."

"What of the third? Can we pay? Do we have coins? I don't have much," Ellette said. "I do have a pendant of copper and silver, though. What about you?" she asked, looking round at the others.

"I've got a few," Lar said, delving into his belt pouch.

Anna followed suit. "A silver nugget and a piece of amber is all I can offer…" she began, holding out the items in the palm of her hand then curling her fingers round them when she saw that Gurthrunn was shaking his head.

"I don't think whoever or whatever is in that room will want mere coins or gems," he said. "After all, if that were the case, the Dweorgar guardians of these treasures could simply pay him, her or it in sufficient quantity *not* to take our bribe. No matter how many coins and valuables we offered it would never be enough."

"Well what else do they want then, if not money?" Lar asked, thrusting his coins back into his pouch.

"'Just that which thee must have that made it possible to enter,'" Gurthrunn quoted. "Whatever do we have that enabled us to enter the catacombs? Think back. How could we six enter, but not the Svartálfar and not Kendra?"

Anna's face had gone pale. "Not that! Surely not that," she said.

"Not what?" Ellette asked.

Her face ashen, Anna stared at the dwarf. "I…I think

the payment would be...our souls. Am I right, Gurthrunn?"

He nodded. "I fear so. A simple payment, huh! There will be a demon or wight or some other creature from the darkness of Hel's domain. If one of us gives up a soul to it then we can proceed."

"Could we not fight it?" Lar suggested weakly.

"Possibly, but then we would risk losing more than one of us."

"Well then, let's not go that way," Lar said.

"So the second room, then," Anna said, "the one beloved of birds. But which is the second? The inscriptions look to be identical."

"Are they, though?" Wilburh murmured, wandering up and down the corridor, studying the three inscriptions. After examining them closely, he shook his head. "Not quite identical. On each of them one rune is larger and more deeply engraved compared with the others. I thought at first it was simply an error, but when you look closely you can see that in each of the inscriptions the rune concerned is one of three: the Tiw rune, which can represent air, for the skies are where the gods live, the Lugaz rune, which stands for water, and the third, the Hagalaz rune, which can mean disaster or destruction."

Gurthrunn came forward and studied the stones one by one. Then he patted Wilburh on the shoulder. "Well spotted, my lad. My old eyes had not seen that."

"So then, which way do we go? Which door leads to the air room?" Ellette asked.

"The one with the Tiw rune." Wilburh pointed at the middle door and the little girl scampered over and bent to listen at it again. A moment later she turned and shook her head. "Still can't hear anything."

"Go ahead and open it," Anna told her, coming to stand

behind her, sword and shield at the ready.

Nodding, the dark-haired girl produced her tools, fiddled with the lock, and in a few moments there was the expected click. She popped her tools away and looked up at Anna. "Ready?" she asked.

Anna nodded.

"Then here we go." Ellette opened the door a fraction and peeped inside.

"Oh dear," she said, swinging the door fully open and standing back as the others each shuffled forward to take a look.

"Woden be merciful!" Lar said, swallowing hard.

The door had opened onto a large chamber, some fifty paces wide and deep. Unlike the other rooms where the ceiling was maybe twelve or fifteen feet above the floor, the roof here soared into the distance at least fifty yards above them. As for the floor, even by craning their necks to look downwards it could not be seen. The room appeared to be bottomless. It fell away seemingly into oblivion, or at least far down into some deep, dark cleft that plummeted out of sight.

"What about the walls, are there any handholds?" said Lar, his gaze flicking around the room.

Ellette shook her head. "No, they seem to be as smooth as ice. I can't see a single handhold between here and that doorway." She pointed across the room.

In the opposite wall they could now see a door matching the one they had opened. Above the lintel was the statue of a stone eagle projecting out into the room, its wings unfurled as if in flight. Wilburh craned his neck and saw that there was another above the doorway where they stood.

Anna, also looking up at the statue, glanced back at Gurthrunn. "Your people are telling us that only an eagle can cross this space...and I have to agree with them," she commented.

"So what do we do now?" Hild asked.

"We will have to go another way. Try the water door, Ellette," Anna suggested.

The little girl looked a question at Wilburh, who pointed towards the right-hand door. "That one."

"No sooner said than done." She grinned and, clutching her bandaged stomach, sprinted off down the hall. As she came in sight of the door she stopped dead, gasped, then turned back and beckoned urgently to Gurthrunn. "Come and see," she called, indicating with a wave of her hand that the others come too.

They hurried to her side and stared in amazement at the wall, for where the door had been only moments ago there was now a solid stone slab sealing off the doorway.

"It must have dropped down when we opened the door to the air room," Gurthrunn said. "'From Three Ways you may choose, and wisely choose you must. But once a way is chosen none other may you take,'" he quoted. "That's what the engraving said and this is what it meant. As soon as one door is opened a mechanism seals off the other two. The other routes are now closed to us, which means there is only the single route. Somehow we must learn to fly!"

They returned to the middle door and looked again on the yawning chasm and the impossible leap. They stood for a long moment in silence, then Hild asked a question.

"Did anyone think to bring some rope?" She looked around at their faces.

In answer, Lar grinned at her and lifted up his tunic to reveal some rope knotted like a wide belt round his waist. "It's what the dark elves used to tie us up. I gathered it up when they weren't looking. It's cut in lengths, of course, but

I thought it might come in useful even so."

"That was well done." Anna smiled at her brother.

"How long is it if we tie the lengths together?" asked Hild. "Could we climb down, do you think? If we use the rope, I mean. Maybe we can find a way across lower down," she suggested.

Lar was shaking his head. "Climb down how far?" he asked. "We can't see the bottom."

"How *long* is it?" Hild repeated, tapping her foot.

The answer, when they checked, was disappointing. "It's not enough, is it," Hild said, rejecting her suggestion. "We could just get as far as dangling at the edge of a bottomless pit. Sorry, Lar. Forget the rope idea."

"Now wait a moment, don't be so hasty to throw your idea away," Lar said, a smile creeping over his face.

"It looks like you've just had another one," Ellette commented.

He grinned at her. "I think there's enough rope to bridge the gap, if only just, and I think I have a way to get it across. I can tie it to a thread and attach it to an arrow. You carry thread in your pouch, don't you, Hild?"

She nodded. "A bit."

"It won't need much. I am sure I can get an arrow to carry the rope and drop it behind the eagle's wings, and it would be easy enough to tie our end to the nearest pillar."

"All well and good, but that's not the issue, is it?" Anna murmured, spelling out the problem. "How do we secure it at the far side, Lar? We don't have enough rope, or thread for that matter, to pull it back across."

They gazed glumly at one another for a moment. "Well we've got to do something, we don't have much time left," Anna said, looking at Wilburh. "I don't suppose...can you help? Can you make the rope coil round the eagle, Wilburh?"

He frowned. "I...I'm not sure." He hesitated, looking at Gurthrunn and not at Anna.

"Try, lad, try," Gurthrunn encouraged him. "Remember what we talked about. The power comes from *you*."

Wilburh shrugged. "Very well...I will try," he said, not sounding very hopeful.

Lar and Gurthrunn knotted one end of the rope round the nearest pillar, pulling on it to ensure it was secure. Then Lar prepared an arrow, tying a thread to the shaft just in front of the flight feathers and securing it to the other end of the rope. Notching the arrow to his bow, he braced himself at the door and aimed up at the ceiling so that the flight would loop upwards and then plummet to earth. He took a deep breath and then let fly. Pulling the rope behind it, the arrow fell a good way short of the eagle and plummeted into the dark chasm at their feet.

"Woden's bones," muttered Lar, clutching the rope and pulling on it hand over hand until the arrow reappeared, still firmly attached by Hild's thread. Lar reloaded his bow and tried again, cursing under his breath when the arrow bounced off the eagle's head and fell short. The third time it flew true, falling beyond the eagle so that the rope lay across the bird's great stone wings. "Got it!" he said. Turning to Wilburh, Lar winked at him and stepped away. "Your turn."

Still feeling that it was pointless to try, Wilburh gulped as he came to the doorway. He brought out the rune sticks and looked down at them. Gurthrunn had suggested he was doing magic wrong in that he had been reaching out and using the dregs of power left in the sticks, but now they were almost drained. *Can I find within me the power to do what I must do?* he asked himself. *Or will there be enough left in the sticks?*

There was only one way to find out. Looking up from

118

the rune sticks, Wilburh stared at the knotted rope that now stretched through the door and across to the eagle statue. The end with the arrow still attached dangled down from where it had lodged on the wings and was swinging back and forth some thirty feet below the bird's stone claws. Keeping the image in his mind, he closed his eyes and searched for the power. He could feel, warm in his hand, what was left of the power in the sticks, but he knew that was not where he was supposed to be looking. He turned his gaze inwards and was disappointed in what he found. He felt hollow – a void as black and empty as the chasm beneath him. There was nothing there. Not even a spark; nothing, apart from despair.

"Wilburh?" Lar prompted.

Realising that he had been standing for too long at the edge of the door, Wilburh opened his eyes, nodded at Lar, then stared at the rope again. There was nothing else to be done except use whatever power was left in the sticks. He reached out for it and felt it, faint and dwindling like the heat in stones that had been left near a dying fire. He drew on it, directed it and summoned the words that cast the spell.

"*Abéonne rápas!*" he shouted.

Across the chasm the rope twitched once, then twitched again, and slowly, as if lifted by an invisible hand, a loop of the rope coiled upwards, moved under the bird and then over the far wing. The loose end snapped back across the top of the eagle, wound around the first wing and then twisted round the bird's head three times before tucking away under the first stretch of rope. A little surprised that the power in the sticks had been enough, Wilburh tugged on the rope. It tightened slightly around the distant bird and then held firm. He turned back and moved away to see them all watching him appreciatively.

"Well," Ellette said, "I guess this is my job now."

Lar shook his head. "You can't. You were cut to shreds in that blade room and are in no fit state to make the crossing. What about you, Gurthrunn?"

Ellette spoke before the dwarf could answer. "He may be smaller than you, Lar, but he's much heavier. I am the smallest and lightest. It has to be me. If the rope will not take my weight, it certainly won't take his, yours, or anyone else's for that matter. It's up to me to test it out."

"I don't care." Lar folded his arms, his face set hard. "Anna – you tell her."

Anna shrugged. "Actually she is right, Lar. She is the lightest, not to mention the most agile. She climbs trees like a squirrel. You know that."

Looking from one to the other, Ellette nodded and grinned up at Lar.

"Oh, very well," he said, giving in, "but just you be careful, Little Elf."

As he stepped away from the door to give the girl room, Anna leant close to him and whispered, "You seem very keen on looking after Ellette all of a sudden."

"She is the smallest. Needs looking after, that is all," Lar said quickly.

His sister winked at him. "Of course that is all there is to it," she teased.

"I don't know what you mean," Lar said, moving away from her, his face reddening.

Anna glanced at Hild and the two of them giggled.

Meanwhile, Ellette had approached the rope. Despite her earlier confidence, Wilburh could see she was afraid, her gaze darting to the bottomless drop. For a moment he thought she would turn away, but suddenly she was off. She wrapped her legs around the rope, letting herself drop down under it and then pulling herself away from the doorway. The rope creaked and stretched under her weight, but Wilburh's knots held. Wincing, she steadily hauled herself hand over hand across the rope.

When the little girl was half way there and doing well, she gave a sudden yelp of alarm and pain. Her hands opened and she let go of the rope, her body dropping violently away so that she ended up dangling from her legs and staring straight down into the yawning depths beneath her.

Everyone gasped in shock. Lar took a few steps towards the room, then stood on the edge of the chasm, looking on helplessly. "I shouldn't have let her go," he moaned.

"Come on, Daughter of Midgard, you can do it," Gurthrunn shouted gruffly, his face filled with anxiety.

For a long time Ellette swung back and forth, and it seemed that she must let go and tumble to her death on some jagged rock that no doubt waited for her far below. None of her companions dared to speak – each paralysed, frozen to the spot, unable to help, unable even to breathe.

Finally, with an almighty effort and a shout of pain, the little girl forced her body to curl back up towards the rope. Stretching out her arms, she grabbed hold of it, hung there for a moment, and then was off again. At the doorway the others all let out the deep breath they had each been holding and watched Ellette haul herself the remaining few yards to the statue.

"Well, now we know the rope will take Ellette's weight, but what about ours?" Hild murmured. "And even if it does, how will we get the weapons and shields over? Supposing…"

"One problem at a time, girl," Gurthrunn growled.

Hild subsided into silence, her gaze on Ellette. Having reached the far side, the little girl scrambled around the eagle and, with her legs wrapped round its head, hung down her full length to grasp the door handle, turning it and pushing the door open and away from her.

As the door opened there was a groaning noise in the floor beneath their feet. The children watched in astonishment as a stone ledge emerged from the wall beneath them. Simultaneously, from a matching location on the far wall another ledge appeared. The two moved slowly closer until, with a loud snap, the two halves slammed together. And now the room had a floor.

"Well done, Little Elf!" Lar shouted, grinning with relief and delight.

Now perched on top of the eagle's head, she grinned

back at him, but her eyes were stark with pain.

"Me first," said Lar to the others in a voice that brooked no argument.

Gathering up their weapons and packs, they watched as Lar stepped tentatively out onto the new floor.

It held.

Without a backward glance, he walked across the room. Hild and Anna followed, then Gurthrunn, and at the back, feeling despondent despite the progress they were making, a very gloomy Wilburh.

# Chapter Fourteen

## Treasures of the Gods

The door Ellette had opened led into yet another many pillared hall, which appeared to be the mirror of the one from which they had entered the chamber of air. They emerged through the centre of three doors. The other two, they surmised, led back into the remaining challenge rooms they had avoided.

"We should stop here and rest before we go on," Hild announced, looking at Ellette. "I'm tired, and Ellette is completely exhausted. And anyway, I must check her wounds. All that exertion might have started them bleeding again."

"Do we have time?" asked Ellette. "What about Raedann? You don't have to stop just because of me, I can manage."

"It's not just you, Little Elf," said Lar, "we're all tired. Unless we get some rest we'll not be in a fit state to confront whatever happens next, and if we're killed, then where will Raedann be?"

"He's right, for once." Anna smiled at her brother. "We must all get some rest – and some food." She turned to Gurthrunn, who nodded.

"I agree. You must conserve your strength for the challenges to come. They will not get any easier. It must by now be late in the afternoon and we have until midday tomorrow, so yes, I think we must rest for a while, but first let us make sure this is a safe place to stop."

While Hild re-dressed Ellette's wounds in the dim light cast by the flickering sconces, the others dropped their packs in a heap and explored the large and apparently empty chamber. They inspected the doors on the far side, only one of which looked as if it could be opened, but they did not try it. When they returned to pronounce it safe, it was to find that Hild and Ellette had unpacked the smoked meats, bread, cheese, apples and weak ale that they had brought with them from Midgard. And so they piled up their shields and weapons and sat down to eat. After this they settled down to rest, Gurthrunn having told them he would stay awake to watch the room.

Sitting on the stone floor, his back against a pillar, Wilburh closed his eyes and tried to sleep, but try as he might, he found he could not drop off. His head was too busy. All he could think about was the problem he was having with magic. Following Gurthrunn's advice, he had tried to dig down deep inside himself and find this hidden power: this mystical strength which he so badly needed. He had failed. The others thought he could do magic, but he could not. He was a fraud. Everything he had done had been using borrowed power, nothing more, and the rune sticks must be completely drained now after the magic with the rope. He had been able to bluff his way thus far, but what now? How could he help the others deal with Kendra? Could he use magic? Would he be able to? Assuming that he survived this adventure, what was he to do about taking back the Vanir's powerful magic to help protect his village? That was the entire reason they had come to Vanaheim after all. Was that now even possible?

He considered talking again to Gurthrunn about the problem, but the dwarf warrior looked tired and full of worry and concerns, and Wilburh did not want to bother him further about his own difficulties. So instead, he slid further down the pillar until he was stretched out on the cold floor, turned over and, using his pack as a pillow, tried to blank his mind and fall asleep. It seemed to take forever, yet he must eventually have dropped off because he was suddenly aware that Lar was shaking his shoulders and telling him to wake up.

"Come on, sleepy, it's time to carry on," Lar was saying. Around them the others were reordering their packs and arming themselves once more. Blinking sleep from his eyes and yawning, Wilburh checked on the useless rune sticks in his belt pouch, slung his pack on his back and, retrieving his seax, slid it into his belt. In the meantime, the others had gathered up their belongings and were all waiting for him, Hild with an anxious look in her eyes.

They walked across the hall to the far side where, as with the previous hall, there were three doors. The difference here was that the left-hand and right-hand doors seemed to be slabs of stone and were devoid of any handle or keyhole. The middle door, however, did have both handle and lock, and this Ellette, who looked a lot better after food and rest, now attempted to pick. She set to work with her customary self-confidence, yet after a few moments it was clear that this lock was rather more complicated than the ones she had already opened in the other rooms, and certainly harder than the simple locks back in Scenestane. Ellette began to look worried as she manoeuvred the lock picks around and around in the lock, beads of sweat appearing on her forehead. Gurthrunn cleared his throat and slipped his war hammer out of his belt, perhaps preparing to try and batter the door down. He stepped forward, but before he could say anything, there was a satisfying click from the door.

Ellette flashed them her habitual, but in this case slightly relieved, smile before opening it. Turning back to the door, she glanced through the opening. As she did so her smile dropped from her face and an expression of profound awe replaced it.

"Merciful Woden, but will you look at this!" she said, her voice shaking.

The others moved past her and stared through the open doorway. The chamber beyond stretched far away from them and seemed to be larger and more brightly lit than the pillared room in which they stood. The walls were lined with shelves, while dotted around in the body of the room were long altar-like stone tables. In front of the shelves along one side were two or three bench seats and a set of wooden steps that had clearly been used by the Dweorgar guardians to access the higher shelves. All were laden, as were the tables, with wondrous treasures of silver and gold that glittered in the light from the wall-hung sconces. Others were fashioned from the most beautiful wood or crafted from the finest bronze or copper.

"Merciful Woden!" Lar echoed.

"We have found it!" Gurthrunn croaked, and in a voice that wobbled with emotion and pride, he added, "Many of these artefacts were fashioned by the greatest craftsmen of my people." He led them into the chamber, passing racks holding weapons of stupendous beauty – magnificent swords, mighty bows or spears of such size that only a god could wield them.

"Look at these," Ellette said, pointing at tunics and gowns of fine silk, embroidered and picked out with silver and gold thread. She reached out and caressed the fabric.

"They are so light and soft!" she purred.

Beyond them was a table holding hundreds of glass vials, each with a runic symbol upon it. Hild examined several of them, lifting lids and sniffing the contents. "I think these must all be potions of healing, strength and life. What I would give for a day to study them," she said, awed.

"We haven't got a day," Wilburh said tersely, coming up behind her. "By now we've got barely half a day. Don't forget why we are here."

"Look at this bow!" Lar exclaimed. He was holding a well-crafted bow with a double curve and the finest workmanship. "I wager an arrow from this could reach 500 paces."

"You were not thinking of taking it, were you?" Wilburh asked, glaring at him. I cannot believe these treasures are sitting here all unprotected, he thought, looking nervously around the chamber, half expecting some monster elemental to erupt from the walls, or a hole to open up in the ground and swallow them. Then, when he thought back over the obstacles they'd had to overcome just to get this far, 'unprotected' did not seem the right word.

Entranced by so many riches, Lar was oblivious to Wilburh's fears. He shrugged. "Why not? I am sure the gods won't miss just one bow."

Anna tutted at her brother. "Remember, we are not here as thieves," she reprimanded him. "We want three items and three alone: the falcon cloak and the jar for Kendra, and the sword for Ullr. We find them, and then…"

Her voice trailed off, because at that precise moment a loud clanging, as if someone or something was striking a huge gong, sounded from somewhere in the room. The noise spread out through the stone and the floor vibrated under their feet.

"What is *that*?" Lar shouted over the noise.

"An alarm! Quick, check the room outside," Gurthrunn yelled.

Lar and Wilburh ran out of the treasure chamber back into the pillared hall. They glanced around, searching for signs of movement, but it still seemed to be empty and silent, apart from the fading echo of the gong.

"If it was an alarm, it seems there is no watch dog," Lar commented, but before Wilburh could answer there was a sound of stone scraping against stone.

"Look over there!" Wilburh pointed. "Look at the doors!"

At either end of the hall the two stone doors were sliding upwards to reveal dark chambers beyond. For a moment there was silence, and then something stirred in the darkness. At first there were only vague, shadowy outlines of figures, but suddenly, in a deep roar of voices, there burst forth from each door three Dweorgar warriors, shouting the familiar war cry: "*Nidarvellir!*"

Just like Gurthrunn, they were armoured in chain shirts and wielded fearsomely large hammers or axes. And just like him, they had the battle frenzy about them, their eyes wide and mouths open in a shout of rage as they charged towards Lar and Wilburh.

# Chapter Fifteen

## Guardians of the Treasures

"Get back!" Lar yelled as he moved towards the treasure room door. He took a few steps, and then spotted that Wilburh was not following him and instead was staring at the oncoming Dweorgar. Swearing under his breath, Lar grasped him by the tunic and dragged him along as he retreated into the treasure chamber. Then, turning to the others, he shouted, "Trouble. Your people are here, Gurthrunn, and they don't look happy!"

"Quickly, shut the door! It'll be the guardians," the dwarf bellowed.

Lar rushed to do so, and in a trice Gurthrunn was beside him. Both leant their weight to the door just as the warrior dwarves slammed against the opposite side. Lar and Gurthrunn staggered back and the door began to give, but with a huge roar Gurthrunn barged his shoulder into it and slammed it shut once more. Dwarf and boy now held the door closed.

"Lock it!" Gurthrunn ordered Ellette through gritted teeth.

The small girl scampered over and fumbled with her picks until a moment later there was a click. "They must have a key, though," she muttered. "Unless..." Flashing a grin at Lar, she shoved one of her picks deep into the lock then bent it rapidly back and forth until the bronze stem snapped, jamming the keyhole and thus preventing the guards from unlocking the door.

"Well done, Little Elf, that was quick thinking," said Lar as he and Gurthrunn stepped back to catch their breath. There was a thump and a bang on the door, but it held.

"It won't keep them out for long," Lar observed, "even with the lock jammed like that. They'll just break the door down. But why don't we simply tell them who we are and what we are after? You're one of them, after all, Gurthrunn."

"I doubt they will listen. These Dweorgar are sworn to protect the treasures. They will only give them up to a Vanir, and the gods are all sleeping. We must find the treasures we came for and then try to escape with them," Gurthrunn replied.

"Escape? How are we supposed to do that?" Lar retorted. "As far as I can see that door is the only entrance and exit from this room."

"I am still considering that problem," the Dweorgar said with a shrug.

The door shook from another heavy blow.

"Maybe you should think faster," Lar observed dryly.

Gurthrunn scowled at him. "They are trying to break down the door, Lar. We don't have time to talk about it. We must act!"

"That's all very well, but..."

Letting out a snort, Anna interrupted whatever Lar had been going to say. She moved to stand between them and frowned. "Stop arguing, you two. We need to find the treasures quickly. Follow me!" So saying, she set off down the room and started to search the shelves as another blow resounded on the door.

"But what do we do then?" Lar asked as he too moved

away from the door and started looking for the treasures.

"Maybe there is another way out of here," Hild suggested. She glanced nervously at the door as another hard blow made it shudder. Grimacing, she turned away and began to sort through the various gorgeous tunics and cloaks that hung from a long free-standing hanger.

"It wouldn't exactly be a secure vault if it had several ways in and out, would it," Lar commented in a dry voice.

"Well maybe we can find something here to help," Anna snapped back. "Do you have to be so sarcastic all the time, Lar?"

"Keep looking!" Gurthrunn shouted at them both, his own voice tense. Then he moved back towards the door and stood there, his huge war hammer and shield at the ready. "Wilburh, come here!"

Wilburh had been sorting through the swords that lay upon a table. He ran over to join the dwarf. There was another thump at the door, and then another and another. It seemed the guardians had found a ram of some sort and were intent on hammering the door down. Yet, at present the lock – fashioned by skilled dwarven hands and jammed by Ellette – was holding.

"I have a question for you," Gurthrunn said.

"What?" Wilburh grunted.

Gurthrunn studied him. "You have not yet worked out why you can't do magic, have you."

Glancing at him, Wilburh scowled. "How do you know?"

"We dwarves know magic. We may not wield it like the gods. Rather, we embed it in sword and gem, but we do know about magic. When you manipulated the rope you drained the last of the power in the sticks, didn't you."

Wilburh looked around to see if the other children were listening, but they were all searching the chamber for the three items they needed to find, and even without the noise from the other side of the door, were too far away to hear the conversation.

"I tried to find the strength within me like you said, but I could not. So all I could do was what Iden taught me and channel the power of the gods through the rune sticks."

"But you are not a priest of the gods, boy. If you are anything, you are a sorcerer. The gods grant power to their clerics as needed to heal and to bless, but that is not what you are trying to do, is it. You wish for the power to manipulate the elements and the ability to control the arcane. Such strength does not flow from the gods. It comes from within you. That is if you truly possess, as I believe, a sorcerer's power."

"I...don't think I do."

"Oh, I believe you do, lad." Gurthrunn tapped Wilburh's chest. "It is in there, the power – deep and untapped. Locked away like these treasures around us. You need to find the way to unlock it, and then like a flood it will come."

"How? How do I unlock it? How do I control it?"

Gurthrunn did not answer. He was staring at the door. The last impact had been so immense that one of the hinges must have given way and the door had buckled. The other two hinges and the lock were holding, but it was clearly only a matter of time before the whole door collapsed.

"Anna, come here. Bring your shield. Lar, string your bow. Wilburh, get behind me – if there ever was a time to find that power, now would be it!"

Anna and Lar ran back towards the door. Anna hefted her shield and stood next to Gurthrunn, her sword at the ready. Lar, reaching for the bowstring in his belt pouch as he ran, strung his bow in one practised movement, his fingers a blur. Then, pulling it taut, he notched an arrow and took his place between Gurthrunn and his sister, half-protected by their overlapping shields since it was not possible for him to hold one of his own while using his bow.

"What about Hild and me?" Ellette called out.

"You keep looking for the treasures!" Anna shouted before Gurthrunn could answer. The dwarf, his war hammer clutched in his fist, nodded, but did not take his gaze from the door.

"Brace yourselves!" he cried as the next impact ruptured another of the hinges. The upper half of the door was shattered and the iron-reinforced heavy oak panel hung inwards. Through the opening they could see the helmeted heads and armoured shoulders of half a dozen dwarven warriors, their faces fierce, sweat dripping from their foreheads from the effort of swinging a battering ram.

One of the guardians stepped forward and peered into the room, taking in Gurthrunn, the figures of the three children with him, and then the two girls searching the treasure chamber behind them.

"What is this?" he growled. "Children of Midgard in the service of one of my kin? A traitor using these humans to get past our wards! You will die for this – all of you."

"Wait!" shouted Gurthrunn. "I am Dweorgar. I serve the Æsir. I am here on a mission for them and for the Vanir."

The guardian captain frowned. "What lies are these? You are clearly servants of that fallen Valkyrie – of Kendra. Through foul sorcery she has trapped our masters, and now sends you to pillage treasures that are not hers to take."

"That's not true. Kendra is our enemy too," Anna shouted. "We defeated her in my village and came here to seek aid from the Vanir."

"You are stealing the treasures!"

"We are not trying to *steal* the treasures," Lar protested. "Er...that is, we just need to borrow some for a bit," he added weakly.

"*Borrow?*" roared the guardian.

"Oh, nicely put, brother," Anna hissed at Lar, who blushed.

At that moment Hild came running back to the group near the door, a long cloak draped over her arms. The garment appeared to be made of some type of fur that had been stitched with a dense layer of falcon feathers. "Found it!" Hild said brightly. "One down and two to go..."

"BORROW!" the guardian roared again. His eyes narrowing, he glared at Hild, then stepped back and prepared to use the ram once more.

"Oops!" said Hild, backing away.

The dwarves swung the ram one last time and now the entire door shattered, sending fragments of wood and iron in all directions. For a moment the guardians stood in the doorway, ram in hand, and then they dropped it and drew hammers and axes.

"Charge!" the guardian captain roared, already moving towards them.

Ellette, who had joined them and had retrieved her sling, released a stone, which smacked one of the warrior dwarves on his chest, but bounced off his chain shirt, leaving no obvious injury. Lar let fly with an arrow, which managed to find an unarmoured spot below the shoulder of the same guardian. This at least slowed the dwarf down; he roared with pain, letting go of his axe, one hand clutching at his wounded shoulder.

Then the remaining guardians were upon them. Too close now to use his bow, Lar dropped it and drew his seax. A mighty swing brought a war hammer down onto Anna's shield, sending her staggering backwards several steps before she could regain her balance and stab back with her own blade, slashing a deep wound across a guardian's forearm. Another had reached Gurthrunn and the two of them, war hammers locked together, were pushing with all their might, each trying to force the other one back.

The guardian captain let out a cry of rage as he advanced on Hild, who was still standing to one side, falcon cloak in her arms. Seeing the dwarf approaching his twin, Wilburh stepped in the way.

"Leave her alone, you coward!" he shouted.

The guardian's eyes bulged at the insult. Then he reached out, seized Wilburh by the tunic and tossed him across the room as if he were nothing more than a *francisca* – a throwing axe.

Wilburh slammed into a stone table and shouted as pain shot down his side. He tried to get up, but another stab of pain in his chest sent him into a heap on the floor.

Lifting up one shaking hand, he directed it at the captain. "*Heoruflá æledfýr,*" he shouted, tensing for the blast of fire he hoped would follow. But...nothing happened.

The guardian captain gave him a dismissive glance and turned back to Hild, who seemed frozen to the spot.

"Give me that cloak!" he roared.

Hild shook her head. "No! We need it for a friend."

"I said, give it to me!" He slammed one mailed fist into Hild's shoulder. With a groan of pain, she stumbled to the ground.

Seeing his twin sister hurt and whimpering on the ground, Wilburh felt anger kindle within him. No, it was more than anger now: it was a red mist of rage – not for himself, but for Hild. He felt an uncontrollable desire to strike back at the one who had hurt his twin. The need to protect her ran deep, but more than that, he felt a need to protect *all* of them. All his friends: Anna, Lar, Gurthrunn and Raedann, and his village too. These dwarves were in the way and that had to end. And it had to end right now.

"STOP!" Wilburh cried, struggling to his feet.

When nobody took any notice, his rage increased, becoming like a pot boiling over on a hearth when the pressure forces the lid off. He felt like one of the distant mountains of fire Raedann had once described in a story. The pressure was mounting within him along with the rage. All he had to do was release it and he knew he would erupt like a volcano.

Without even thinking about it, the boy sorcerer spread

out his hands, and from deep within him the power surged –
not drawn from the gods, not hidden in mere pieces of wood,
but drawn from deep within his spirit. Not like before when
he had merely wanted this power, desired it, and nothing had
happened. Now he did not just want it, he needed it – truly,
really needed it, and in answer to his most desperate need the
power released by his rage came surging like a flood to his
fingertips, just as Gurthrunn had said it would. The feeling
was like nothing Wilburh had experienced before.

"*Ádæle!*" As he shouted the word of command, it was as
if the pot had exploded or the volcano erupted. An invisible
wave of energy burst forth from his hands and shot across
the room. Dwarves and humans alike were knocked onto

their backs. Treasures were scattered around the chamber. Suits of armour crashed to the ground, and heaps of jewels and precious metals were strewn about the floor.

"I said STOP!" Wilburh shouted, and everyone, mostly lying on the ground, turned to stare at him in awe.

"Gods of Æsir and Vanir protect us!" the guardian captain said. Then, slowly getting to his feet, but leaving his hammer on the ground and holding his hands so all could see he was unarmed, he approached Wilburh.

Staring in shock at his own hands, Wilburh, his knees trembling, was gasping for breath. The sudden release of power had left him feeling completely drained and weak.

*I must learn to control it better*, he thought. As the captain neared him, Wilburh looked up, and the dwarf flinched. Recognising the dwarf's fear, Wilburh took a step backwards.

"We are not your enemy," he said. "Can we please talk?"

The guardian captain studied him for a moment and slowly nodded. "After what just happened, I certainly don't want *you* as an enemy! Yes, let us talk."

# CHAPTER SIXTEEN

## NEGOTIATIONS

The captain, who said his name was Hamaal, told the warrior dwarves to lay down their weapons. He then directed them to clear one of the smaller stone tables of treasure and pull up a couple of benches so they could all sit down. With occasional nervous glances at Wilburh, the guardians did as they were told, piling the artefacts onto adjacent shelves.

When everyone was sitting around the now empty table, Hild, who had handed the feathered cloak to Anna, slowly worked her way around all the wounded, dwarves and children, attending to their injuries with her needle and thread, salves and dressings. Apart from the one arrow embedded in a guardian's shoulder, most of the wounds were cuts, grazes and bruises; nothing too serious. While she worked, Gurthrunn, with occasional additions from Wilburh and Anna, told their tale of why they had come to Vanaheim and what they had found when they arrived there. How they had then discovered that Kendra and her army of Svartálfar had captured and bound the Vanir gods and how, having seized their friend Raedann, she had compelled them to agree to find the items she desired.

Hamaal gazed doubtfully at Wilburh. "So you are saying that before he fell asleep, the divine Ullr – without actually

140

speaking – requested that you bring him the blade named Gambantein?"

Wilburh nodded. "As I told you, he spoke directly into my thoughts and asked for our help to free him. He specifically asked me to bring him that sword."

"We believe it might be capable of severing Gleipnir – the golden thread," said Gurthrunn.

The dwarf considered this. "That is possible. Certainly I can think of nothing else that could."

"What of this falcon cloak? What powers does it have?" Anna asked, examining the cloak in her hands.

"Do you know whose cloak it is?" Hamaal asked.

Anna nodded and looked across at Wilburh, her eyebrow raised.

"The Goddess Freya?" he suggested.

"Indeed," Hamaal said.

"So Kendra wishes to possess another treasure of Freya's," Anna said with a grimace.

"Another?" Hamaal queried.

"Earlier in the summer, when Kendra briefly took over Scenestane, our village, she was wearing Freya's beautiful necklace..."

"The Brisingamen?"

"Yes. We took it off her, and later, when I met the Goddess Freya in Asgard, I was able to give it back to its rightful owner."

"You met Freya?" The dwarf captain's eyes widened in astonishment, his expression changing to one of respect as he gazed at Anna.

She nodded. "Yes. But what does Kendra want with the cloak? What can it do?"

"The wearer can transform into a falcon. Freya used to use it sometimes to fly over Midgard and choose which mortals dying in battle would go to her afterlife fields rather than to Woden's table in Valhalla," Hamaal answered.

"A nice trick, I am sure," Lar said. "Somehow, though, I figure that Kendra has a bigger plan for it than just becoming a bird. As I recall, she already has a horse that flies, if flying is what she wants to do."

They considered this in silence, but it was clear no one could immediately think what the Valkyrie's plan might be, so Lar went on to ask another question.

"What of this jar that she also wants?"

Hamaal shrugged. "There are many jars and vases here. I believe I have seen the jar you describe, but I do not know what it contains, nor its purpose."

"It seems a bit odd," said Lar, looking around the room. "This chamber contains the treasures of the Vanir, powerful artefacts and great wealth. Why, given a choice of all that, does Kendra ask for this one jar?"

Hild looked up from where she had just removed Lar's arrow from a guardian's shoulder, her hand poised with a needle and thread ready to stitch up the wound. "Maybe we can open it and examine the contents," she suggested.

"No." Hamaal shook his head. "Alas, you cannot. The jars are generally sealed by the Vanir gods when returned to storage, and only they can open them."

"I see," Hild said. With a quick glance at Wilburh, which seemed to say she thought he probably could too, she said nothing more and returned to her work.

Anna put the cloak down on the table and stood up. "Well then, you have heard our tale. We are allies and servants of the Æsir, and at least in the matter of Gambantein also under the commission of the Vanir."

"So you say," Hamaal corrected her. "In fact in all these

matters, so far you have given us no proof. By rights we should detain you until we can confirm all this with the Vanir, but…"

"But the Vanir are prisoners, and Vanaheim is under the control of Kendra and the Svartálfar. Your masters are helpless, and you six, despite your valour and strength, are not enough to rescue them," Anna said.

"Neither could you," Hamaal pointed out.

"No, we could not. But together we are twelve."

"Aside from our kinsman, Gurthrunn, you are just children," Hamaal objected.

"We are children who earlier this year defeated Kendra and freed our village. We are children who have survived your catacombs. I was given this sword by Woden himself," Anna said, lifting up her blade. "And as for Wilburh here…" she smiled across at the boy sorcerer "well, you saw for yourself what he can do."

Hamaal glanced at Wilburh, shivered, and then nodded his head. "Indeed we did."

"So let us unite to defeat Kendra," Anna said. "Let us be allies."

The guardian captain thought about this for a moment and finally he too stood up. "Very well, let me discuss your proposal with the other guardians." He moved to the other end of the table and gathered in a huddle with his warriors.

While they were talking, Gurthrunn leant across to Wilburh. "That – whatever it was – was a remarkable demonstration of power. I take it that whatever was the issue before, you have now resolved it?"

Wilburh shrugged. "I am not sure."

"What do you mean?"

"I mean that I didn't make it happen, not exactly. It

143

just happened when I was desperate to save Hild from her attacker. I know what I felt like: I was filled with rage – angry and protective all at the same time. I just don't know if I can make it happen again, that's all."

Gurthrunn grunted. "Wilburh, you know you have the power now. You know you can release it. Now you must learn how to control it."

Nodding, his brow furrowing in concentration, Wilburh thought deeply about what had happened. Suppose it was just a fluke? Will I be able to make it happen again? he asked himself. And if so, will I be able to control it?

The dwarves' huddle broke up and Hamaal returned to Gurthrunn's end of the table. "Very well, we will fight alongside you – but what is your plan?"

Gurthrunn played with his beard as he considered a reply. "The Svartálfar are numerous and that troll is an additional hindrance. We must engage them both, but the most important aim must be to get the sword to Ullr and free the Vanir gods."

"That will be hard given that Kendra will have the entrance to the catacombs watched. As soon as we emerge it is likely that we will be seized, along with the treasures we are carrying," Anna pointed out.

"The Vanir are locked up in that library, and so is Raedann," Hild put in. "We need to get in there before we hand over the treasures."

Hamaal's face darkened at that. "Hand them over? We cannot permit Kendra to take possession of any of these artefacts. You surely cannot be considering that?"

Anna shook her head. "Of course not, but if we don't go out there with them, she will know we are tricking her and Raedann will be killed."

"I am sorry for your friend," Hamaal said, his face

growing hard, "but my task is to protect the gods' treasures. I cannot risk the possibility that this rogue Valkyrie will lay her hands upon them."

"But don't you see?" Anna exclaimed. "This is how we get close to Ullr with the sword. If we insist on handing the items over only in exchange for Raedann being released, then she will have to take us to the library chamber where he and the gods lie bound."

Hamaal considered this. "Very well then. We use the cloak and pot to get close to the gods. Then we use the sword to free them and defeat Kendra and her servants," he suggested.

Looking thoughtful, Lar was the one to point out the flaws in this plan. "Two things occur to me," he said to no one in particular. "One: Kendra is not to be trusted. She'll more than likely kill us all to get her hands on the artefacts, whatever has been said about an exchange. For all we know she may have already killed Raedann anyway. And two: how are we going to get the guardians into the library without being noticed? As soon as she sees the Dweorgar warriors, Kendra will know it is a trick and will attack us all – and her magic is extremely powerful."

Anna grimaced. "We have to go out first then, don't we. The guardians will have to stay hidden in the catacombs until we find out if Raedann is still alive. We have to hope that he is…" Her voice trailed away, and then she smiled. "I have an idea: maybe Wilburh can threaten to set Freya's cloak on fire unless Kendra agrees to the exchange." She looked at Wilburh. "You could do that, couldn't you?" she said, ignoring Hamaal's horrified gasp of dismay.

Before he could reply, Hild said, "Of course he could, you saw what he is capable of. Maybe he could give Kendra a fright with a little demonstration of his power by setting fire to one of her horrid elves." She grinned at her twin.

Wilburh frowned, then slowly he nodded. "I...I *might* be able to," he said. "Well, I can at least try."

"I'm not sure that is such a good idea," said Gurthrunn. "I believe that your magic will eventually be as powerful as Kendra's – indeed it may be so already, but you have not yet learnt to control it, and the stakes are too high for you to try and fail. We would all be killed instantly."

"Perhaps you're right," said Anna. "So then, we have to hope that Kendra is as good as her word and will exchange Raedann's life for the treasures. With luck that will get us into the library. Once there we will call for the guardians' aid using Hild's horn." She pointed to the horn at Hild's belt, and a distant expression came into her face. "It's not quite the Gjallahorn – which is a pity, for if it was I could summon the Valkyries to our aid." Anna shrugged. "But it is loud," she added wistfully, clearly thinking back to Heimdall's golden horn that she had once used to summon an army of Valkyries. "What I would give for just such an army right now!" she murmured.

Ellette, who had been quiet for quite some time, shook her head. "I don't like it. As soon as Kendra has her hands on the treasures she will have no more use for us or for Raedann. She will kill us all the moment Hild blows her horn."

Hamaal pointed a finger at Wilburh. "I think, then, that this is where your companion can show his talents. Whatever you say, Gurthrunn, surely with a power such as his, the boy sorcerer can keep you safe while we rush to your aid?"

All eyes turned to Wilburh – Hamaal's expression respectful, the children's eager and expectant, for had they not all seen how great a sorcerer he was after all? Gurthrunn, however, was studying him, weighing the boy up, for he alone knew the difficulties Wilburh had experienced.

"Well, boy," he growled, "do you think you can manage that?"

Wilburh stared back at him. What a time to ask a question like that, he said to himself, recalling he had thought exactly the same thing when Nerian had asked the question back in Scenestane. Much had happened since then, of course. Then he had not understood the power he had. All sorts of incorrect ideas had passed through his mind. He had believed the wrong things about the control of sorcery. Iden had taught him to try to draw on the power of the gods as a priest might. That was appropriate for Iden, but as Gurthrunn had pointed out, not for a sorcerer. The dwarf had suggested that he merely needed to find a way to command the power, much as a lord commanded an army. That might work for the Dweorgars, who took power and bound it in the items they made, but once again, not for him.

Deep in thought, Wilburh looked at Hild for a moment – his twin sister. Sometimes they could almost read each other's mind, while at other times they seemed like opposites: two halves of the same person. Hild was the protective one who cared for others and was always there trying to heal and succour everyone. He too wanted to protect the people he loved, but the power was not there to be begged like a supplicant priest, nor commanded like a great warrior. It was not the distant power of the gods or the abstract power of the elements that he possessed. No, the power was there in his soul, burning inside his very spirit. Is anger the key to releasing it? he wondered, knowing that if Kendra threatened his sister and his friends he would be every bit as angry as he had been just now. He needed to give in to it, yield himself and let the power come to him and be part of him, like it had when he really needed it. Indeed it *was* part of him, in the same way that a husband and wife are both two and one at the same time, or a hand becomes one with a glove.

"Well, can you?" Hild asked.

Wilburh shrugged.

"Yes, I believe I can," he answered with a shy smile. "Or rather, I believe *we* can!"

# CHAPTER SEVENTEEN

## EXCHANGE

"This is the chest that contains Gambantein," Hamaal explained with a grunt of effort as he hauled on a handle and pulled an ancient looking dust-covered iron chest into view. It was quite long, and they could all see that it was secured by not one but three locks. On the table nearby, the cloak still lay where Anna had placed it, and next to it stood a large crock pot, about three foot high and bearing a handle on either side, the M rune clearly visible on its front.

One of the other guardians handed Hamaal a set of keys, and he fumbled with them until he found a key that fitted the chest's first lock. It appeared that each of the locks required a different key, and it took some time and more fumbling to unlock all three. Finally, the last one clicked open and Hamaal reached down to open the lid.

"That is a lot of locks for just one sword," Lar observed.

Hamaal glanced at him. "This is not 'just one sword', Child of Midgard. Gambantein is as strong a blade as you can imagine, and more. The fact that it can immolate is impressive..." He paused, seeing Ellette's puzzled frown. "That means burst into flames, child." She nodded, and he continued, "Not only that, it is even able to float in the air and fight by itself for a while. But more even than that, it does not just cut or burn its foes. Gambantein was forged for use in the wars between the Vanir and Æsir long ago, and gods need more than just a bit of slashing and burning to bring them down. The sword was created to drain life force into itself, and as a result it becomes more alive with each foe it slays."

"What do you mean, *alive*?" asked Lar, his face suddenly pale.

"I mean what I say. Gambantein is alive. It is conscious, it thinks and it can speak to its wielder. To a powerful mind it becomes a potent ally in battle. Yet if the being that wields it is weak-willed then the sword will dominate them, taking over their mind until in time that wielder becomes the blade's slave and can no longer control it."

"Merciful Woden!" gasped Ellette. "I can see why they keep the thing locked up."

Hamaal nodded. "Quite," he replied, glancing at Anna, who was smiling. "What amuses you, child?"

"Nothing really, it's just that it reminded me a bit of my own sword. Aefre does not have the same dangerous powers as Gambantein, but the blade seems to speak to me sometimes, and when I fight it feels alive in my hand."

"Ah." Hamaal nodded, bending to open the heavy lid of the chest. "If the Father of all Gods himself gave you your sword then that does not surprise me. You are favoured indeed to own such a weapon."

Despite the dusty and age-worn exterior, the inside of the chest was in very good condition, and indeed was lined with luxurious deep-purple velvet. Lying in the very centre was an item wrapped in cloth. Without touching what lay beneath it, Hamaal gingerly pulled the cloth away to reveal the sword.

Gambantein was indeed a mighty weapon. Clearly

designed to be used one-handed, probably with a shield, the long blade was sheathed in an intricately stitched leather scabbard, as was the hilt, which had its own sheath, close-fitting like a glove.

"That's unusual," Wilburh said, pointing to the hilt.

"Yes." Hamaal nodded. "It is protected thus for it is the actual contact with the hilt that makes the connection between the wielder and the blade."

Gently lifting Gambantein from the chest, taking care to touch only the covered hilt, he slid the sword a few inches out of its scabbard so that they could see the broad black blade. Forged from steel and finely honed, the edges looked wickedly sharp.

Fascinated, Ellette reached out a finger to touch it, but Hamaal grabbed her arm. "No, child!" he exclaimed. "It will burn you. Whatever you do, you must not touch the naked blade. Not if you want to keep your fingers." Pushing it back into its scabbard, he added, "And none of you should handle the hilt either."

"Well then," chirped Ellette, "why can't we handle it with the hilt scabbard on?"

Hamaal shrugged. "For transportation purposes that would be ideal. But if we wish to use the sword and wield its powers, such as we propose doing to sever Gleipnir, this will not be sufficient. Gambantein will not react unless it feels the wielder's hand upon it."

Anna frowned. "Then one of us will *have* to handle it."

"No, not you." Hamaal shook his head. "I must do it."

"You can't. The plan is to get the sword to the library and use it as early as we are able. We cannot wait for you to join us," Anna said.

"Then *I* must do it," Gurthrunn suggested, but Anna disagreed.

"We don't know how long it will take us to free Ullr, or how long it will take for the gods to wake from slumber. We must free them as soon as possible. It should be me. I have used an artefact of the gods before: the Gjallahorn for one, my own sword for another. Admittedly Aefre is nowhere near as powerful, but even so, I know what it feels like to deal with an item of power and life. I can handle it."

Gurthrunn looked anxious. "Anna, for all its power, the Gjallahorn was benevolent, as is your sword. Gambantein was designed as a dark weapon, made darker by many years of service in Jotunheim. We do not know what it can do to a mortal mind. Best if you let me try..."

"No, Gurthrunn! You are as mortal as I am. In any case we will need you to keep the Svartálfar away from us. I will do it."

"But...you are so young. Mortal I am, but I have lived for centuries."

"Gurthrunn, it was you who told my father that my age is not relevant. You can't now twist it around another way. I am doing it and that's an end to it." Anna spoke with finality and the dwarf reluctantly gave in.

The decision made, Hamaal wrapped the sword once more inside the cloth, and with Lar's help strapped it to Anna's back under her cloak and shield, all of it hidden except the end, which protruded a few inches beneath the hem of her cloak.

"Try not to turn your back towards Kendra," said Wilburh. "We'll just have to hope she is so keen to get her hands on the treasures she's asked for that she won't notice."

"I'll take your pack, Anna," said Lar. "It's practically empty, I can fold it inside mine." Shoving one pack inside the other, he slung it on his back with his bow. Then, adjusting the strap of his quiver so that it hung across one shoulder, he quickly gathered up his spent arrows from where they had fallen in the fight, discarding any that were damaged. "Right, I'm ready," he announced. "Let's go."

Then, with Hild carrying the feathered cloak, Ellette and Wilburh each taking one handle of the pot, and Anna, Lar and Gurthrunn bringing up the rear, Hamaal and the other guardians led the way back through the broken door and into the pillared hall.

"I am sure it must be morning by now," Hild said. "Suppose we don't get back in time?"

"Do we have to go back through the catacombs? I am not sure I can face that wheel trap again," Ellette piped up.

Hamaal shook his head. "No, we don't need to go that way," he replied. "This way is much quicker." He led them through one of the stone doors by which he and the guardians had entered the hall when the alarm gong had sounded. The moment they were all through, he pressed a carved rune in the wall and the stone doors both closed. "They can't be opened from the other side," he said.

"We'd noticed," commented Lar.

Beyond the doors they followed the guardians past the dwarves' own chambers, store rooms, workshops and repair rooms, and finally into a narrow corridor that led all the way around the outside of the catacombs. From here they passed through a small concealed door in the side wall, and in moments were standing in the wide main passageway, just beyond the first set of inner doors that led into the chamber with the oak table. They were mere yards from the main entrance and it had taken barely any time at all.

"I did not see this door before," Lar commented. "I could have saved us all a good deal of trouble if I had."

"Of course you did not see it," Gurthrunn said smugly.

"Well neither did you," Lar retorted.

The dwarf looked momentarily uncomfortable. "No, if it comes to that, neither did I. My people are masters of hidden doors. And anyway, even if I had spotted it, I doubt we could have opened it from the wrong side."

"You're right," said Hamaal, overhearing. "On both counts," he added with a smile.

They all assembled in the passageway between the inner and outer doors. "Before you open the main door, we guardians will go back into the corridor so we are hidden from view until you have exited. Never fear, we will be ready and waiting for your call."

"Listen out for my horn," Hild reminded him.

Hamaal nodded, and with the other dwarves retreated back into the corridor, pulling the small door to behind them. Lar blinked. Even though he was staring at the spot, once closed it was impossible to see the door or discern that it had ever been there. Frowning, he touched the rock surface and felt all around, then gave a low whistle.

"Not even an edge or a crack. That *is* impressive!"

Once more looking smug, Gurthrunn led them to the entrance door, which had a set of iron rings matching those on the outer side. As he had done on the previous day, the dwarf heaved on the rings and the doors swung open. By now everyone had acclimatised to the darker environment of the catacombs, whose passageways were only dimly illuminated by torchlight. The bright daylight flooding in through the open doors blinded them all, and for a moment they stood there blinking. Then the world came slowly into focus and they all wished it had not.

Outside the doors seventy or more Svartálfar were camped. Many were sleeping, some cleaning weapons and repairing clothing. Some were roasting what appeared to be a pair of boar, skewered and suspended over a large newly dug fire pit. Most, however, were on their feet and glaring at the mortals, apparently having leapt up when the doors opened and quickly armed themselves. In moments they came swarming towards the six companions.

Anna stepped forward and, pointing to the cloak and pot, said, "We have the items your mistress asked us to bring. Take us to her!"

One of the Svartálfar came forward out of the ranks, and Anna recognised the captain who had captured them on the previous day. He cast his gaze over her and the other children as if surprised to find they had all survived intact. He then stared suspiciously at Gurthrunn. Finally, he inspected the treasures, sniffed at them each in turn, and then, with a sneer at Anna, snarled a command.

"Bring them and come with us."

They walked across the open space behind the Vanir's hall and then circled around it to the front entrance. As before, they were marched along the hall's vast length until once again they stood in front of Kendra, who was lounging on her stolen throne.

"Well, well. So, you have *all* managed to stay alive," she sneered. "What a pity. I trust you have the items I need?"

In answer, Hild held up the cloak, and Wilburh and Ellette the pot.

"You will give them to me right now," she said, "or you will die." She beckoned several of the Svartálfar forward. They rushed to do her bidding, thrusting with their spears, the sharp points stopping only inches from the three children. Gurthrunn took a step towards them and raised his war hammer.

"No, Gurthrunn!" Anna shouted, holding him back. "We cannot win, we will all be killed."

"You are wise, child," said Kendra.

"I thought we had agreed an exchange," Anna replied hotly.

Tilting back her head, the Valkyrie laughed out loud.

"We'd best do as she says," murmured Wilburh, staring up into Kendra's laughing face and seeing through her flawless beauty to the evil that lay behind it. He felt his anger stirring, his rage beginning to bubble.

Kendra inclined her head towards two more of her servants, who ran forward and seized the treasures from the children, then turned and delivered them to Kendra, laying

the pot on the floor near the throne and holding the cloak up towards her. Getting to her feet, she waved the dark elves back and stepped down from the throne to examine the cloak. Seemingly satisfied, she laid it on the empty throne that stood beside her own. Then she bent and inspected the pot, her long fingers tracing out the M rune. For a moment her hand drifted up to the lid as if she were about to take it off. The children each leant forward, eager to see what lay within. Yet it seemed that what both she and Hamaal had said was true and only a Vanir God could open it, for a moment later Kendra shrugged and returned to her throne.

"These are indeed the items I needed," she announced, speaking to the assembled dark elves rather than to the children and Gurthrunn.

"Then we are finished here, High One?" queried the dark elf captain.

"Almost," Kendra replied, her gaze now falling upon Anna and her companions. The way she was looking at them was not pleasant.

"We did as you asked us, Kendra. A bargain is a bargain. Now will you take us to the library, free Raedann and let us go home?" Anna asked.

The Valkyrie smiled at them. It was, however, a smile devoid of any warmth: the type of smile reserved for enemies, not friends. "You fools! You have brought all that I needed. You and your tinker are of no more use to me. I can finally have my revenge for my defeat at your pitiful village, and at the same time be rid of your interfering pet dwarf." She turned to the waiting packs of Svartálfar gathered around her throne.

"Guards," she commanded, "kill them all!"

# Chapter Eighteen

## Battle of Vanaheim

The Svartálfar began moving towards Gurthrunn and the children, drawing their curved knives, eyes glinting with excitement and anticipation of what they were about to do.

"Treacherous snake!" Gurthrunn snarled at Kendra, hefting his war hammer and threatening to smash down any dark elf who came near him.

The Valkyrie simply laughed at the insult and waved her army forward.

"We need to get to the library and free the gods!" Anna whispered, drawing her sword and heaving her shield into position as she backed away from the advancing Svartálfar.

At her side, Gurthrunn nodded. "Get ready," he muttered. Stalling for time, he turned to glare at the sorceress. "We had an agreement, Kendra!" he shouted. "We brought you what you asked for in exchange for Raedann. Now release him as you promised."

She laughed in his face. "You surely did not think I would honour that agreement?"

"Apparently not," said Anna as she and the others moved back to form a little cluster in the middle of the hall. Gurthrunn clutched his hammer while Lar readied his bow and Ellette her sling. Hild held her seax in one hand, the other resting on the horn at her belt.

Of them all, Wilburh made no move to arm himself and nor did he reach for the rune sticks. His eyes dark, he studied the Svartálfar while he brought together all the thoughts and feelings he had experienced over the last few days. "I do not serve the power," he said to himself. "Neither is the power my servant. We are one, and together we will protect our friends and defeat our foes."

The dark elves surged around them until they were surrounded and then started moving inwards, drawing the circle tighter, all the while snarling at the companions.

"Hild, the horn!" Gurthrunn hissed. "Blow the horn."

Pulling the ox horn from her belt, Hild placed it to her lips and, taking a deep breath, blew as hard as she could. A loud blast echoed around the wooden hall.

Kendra frowned. "What are you doing? Calling for help?" She looked towards the far doors. "From whom?"

By way of an answer Hild blew once more. Then Anna stepped forward and showed the dark elves her sword. "See this? It is no ordinary sword. It was forged in Asgard, created by Wayland, blacksmith to the gods, and given to me by Woden himself. Which of you would like to feel its bite first?"

As they hesitated, the shield maiden turned to her companions and bellowed, "CHARGE! Run for the library!"

Anna and Gurthrunn, followed closely by Wilburh, hurtled towards the library door, aiming to crash straight through the swarming ring of dark elves, but they were numerous and Anna knew she and her companions would have a tough fight to break out in any direction. Yet, in the moment before she and Gurthrunn reached the Svartálfar, Wilburh thrust out one hand and shouted, "*Æledfýr blæstas!*"

A plume of fire erupted from his fingertips and enveloped half a dozen dark elves. The fierce heat of the flames singed

Gurthrunn's beard and scorched Anna's cheek as it passed on by. Caught in the centre of the blast where the heat was most intense, the six Svartálfar burst into flames and fell to the ground, turned instantly into just so many charred skeletons.

Everyone stopped moving and there was a moment's shocked silence.

"Merciful Woden!" Ellette gasped.

First to recover, Anna and Gurthrunn thrust forward again and reached the still smoking gap in the ring of dark elves. Anna turned to one side, her sword a blur as she slashed and cut back and forth. One elf fell screaming to the ground, and the others, still stunned by the blast of fire and clearly terrified by her sword, backed off. Gurthrunn meantime had turned to his right and swung his mighty war hammer, hitting two dark elves full in the chest and sending them flying back into the ranks behind, knocking more of them over onto their backs.

"Get past them!" Anna yelled. The children scampered through the gap. Lar turned as he passed his sister and, still running, sent an arrow across the ring of Svartálfar, killing one. Ellette was first to reach the library door, but Lar and Wilburh were soon beside her. Lar then turned to shout back at Anna.

"Come *on*, Anna! Bring Gambantein!"

She nodded and backed towards them. Gurthrunn followed her, forming a rear guard as the shield maiden headed towards the library doorway.

"Hush, Lar, we don't want Kendra to know what we are doing!" Anna hissed with a glance towards the throne. But it was already too late. The Valkyrie had stood to watch the fight and was now glaring at her. A moment later she leapt down from her seat.

"STOP THEM!" she shouted, running to join the dark

160

elves as they surged after the children. "Did you not hear them? They have Gambantein! This could wreck everything. Stop them!"

The dark elves attacked again with more vigour. A dozen threw themselves towards Gurthrunn, while more swept past to his left and right, heading towards the doorway.

Lar's hands were a blur as he loaded his bow, fired and reached for another arrow.

As had happened before, Wilburh's initial burst of power had taken a lot out of him, so instead of repeating the huge blast of fire, he sent tiny darts of mystical energy, each one wounding or killing a dark elf. Close by, Hild was using her sling, and while she was certainly not the mistress of it that Ellette was, nevertheless at such short range she was finding a mark and doing some damage with her stones. "Where are the guardians?" she gasped. "Why haven't they come?"

Fifteen elves were down, dead or wounded, but more than fifty remained, and they were now surging at the companions, clearly more frightened of their Valkyrie mistress than of their mortal foes. Sooner or later the bite of their knives and spears would overwhelm the children and Gurthrunn.

"We desperately need help," Anna gasped, "divine help."

"Get the door open!" Lar shouted.

Ellette turned the handle and opened the door, intending to go through. However, one glance at the room beyond and she froze in mid step, paralysed by the sight in the library.

As Wilburh peered over her shoulder, he understood why she had halted. The Vanir gods and Raedann were not alone in the chamber. The library room was filled by at least fifty more dark elves, all armed and clearly waiting in ambush.

"Oh dear," Ellette said as she loaded her sling and swung it around her head, "this is not going to be easy!"

# Chapter Nineteen

## Nidarvellir!

"Attack, Attack! Kill them all!" Kendra screamed.

The dark elves responded with a deafening roar as they began closing in upon Gurthrunn and the children. Ducking and diving to avoid their spears, the companions were pressed back away from the library by the elves crowding out of the doorway, driving them into the oncoming Svartálfar in the throne room.

"We're trapped," cried Ellette, letting fly with her sling. The stone smacked into the forehead of a dark elf with yellow teeth and a scar on his cheek. His eyes glazed over as he collapsed. His companions screeched in rage and several threw javelins towards the girl. She half closed her eyes in anticipation of being hit, but just before the razor sharp points reached her they stopped in mid-flight and fell to the ground as though bouncing off an invisible barrier. A moment later the charging mass of dark elves reached the same barrier. With a crash several smacked straight into it, just as if they had run full tilt into a stone wall. They fell about screeching with pain. Seeing this, some of their comrades veered away at the last minute, while others ran on, also slamming into the invisible barrier. Still more hobbled away, holding broken wrists, dislocated shoulders and bruised toes. The remainder fled back into the library.

"Ellette, all of you, come back towards me!" shouted Wilburh.

Glancing over her shoulder, Ellette saw that he was standing sideways in the library doorway, one hand pointing into the throne room and the other into the library. His face was taut with concentration. She now realised that the air was shimmering. Then she saw a huge globe surrounding her and the others. Barely visible, almost transparent yet hard as steel, it hung above them, shielding them as they slowly retreated to the library door.

"Clever child," shrieked Kendra. "So you can build an shield. Alas, little boy, it will not hold for long," she sneered. Now it was Kendra who was pointing and reciting arcane words. With a blinding flash and an ear-shattering crack, a bolt of lightning sprang out of her hand and impacted on the shield. The globe suddenly glowed with an incandescent light and then was gone, reminding them all that Kendra was not just a Valkyrie warrior but a sorceress of significant power to equal or even exceed Wilburh's.

"Get back on your feet and attack them!" Kendra commanded her bruised servants, and soon the dark elves were moving eagerly back into the fray, looking for revenge.

Even though it had not lingered for long, Wilburh's shield had given the companions a few moments of respite in which to catch their breaths. "Where *are* those guardian dwarves?" Lar commented, glancing towards the doors at the far end of the throne room.

"Probably having to fight their way through that dark elf encampment outside the catacombs," Gurthrunn replied. "Look out! Here they come again. Anna, take Wilburh and Lar and get to Ullr. He is our only hope. The girls and I will hold the door for as long as we can."

Anna, who had not yet succeeded in gaining enough

time to draw Gambantein from under her cloak, nodded and stepped into the library along with her brother and Wilburh. Gurthrunn moved to stand just beyond the doorway, blocking the entrance but allowing a small amount of space for Ellette and Hild to use their slings and fire around him.

"Come on then, Valkyrie!" he roared "Come and face me." Kendra just laughed and waved her dark elves forward.

Gurthrunn bellowed as he swung his hammer in a half circle, shattering bones and scattering the elves. Others hung back and heaved javelins towards the dwarven warrior. Two bounced off his armour, but one dug deep into his thigh and the Dweorgar went down on one knee. The girls' arms whirled like fury over their heads as they tried to protect Gurthrunn by keeping up a barrage of stones and pebbles from their slings. But the Svartálfar were too many. As soon as one elf fell it was replaced by another, and seeing that the dwarf was now vulnerable, they surged forward, each one desperate to slay him; each wanting to be the one that Kendra would reward. A dozen dark elves now hemmed him in and a dozen curved blades went back, ready to finish the job.

At that moment the great doors of the throne room burst open with a crash that echoed around the walls. Standing in the doorway of the Vanir gods' halls were the six Dweorgar warriors, led by Hamaal. Eyes bright with battle fury and their weapons covered in blood, the guardians looked exhausted from the fight to get this far. Two of them were clearly badly hurt – yet they were here, as they had promised.

"*Nidarvellir!*" Bellowing their war cry, they charged into the hall. Kendra screamed with fury. The dark elves swarming around Gurthrunn turned and many of them now ran towards the oncoming foe. With a crash, the ranks of the Svartálfar met the Guardians of the Catacombs and battle was joined.

Watching the fight, Kendra was circling off to one side. She appeared to be considering the new arrivals and the way the battle had turned. Frowning her disappointment, she reached inside a pouch at her belt and, bringing out a small bone flute, blew a few notes on it. For such a small instrument, the noise it produced was incredibly loud.

To Wilburh it seemed as if there was some signal in that tune – it was a call or summons. If he was correct, that prompted the question: a summons for what?

Meanwhile, still inside the library were twenty dark elves. Recovered from their encounter with Wilburh's invisible barrier, they had gathered again, ready to charge.

Anna did not wait for them. "Lar, watch my back!" she shouted and, sword and shield at the ready, she flung herself at the Svartálfar.

Lar fired arrow after arrow at those who were attempting to lap around his sister on one side, while Wilburh, using a spell a little like Kendra's own, shot bolts of hissing sparking light at those on the far side. In their midst, Anna, Shield Maiden of Scenestane, was using all the skills and tricks Meccus had taught her this summer, along with a few of her own. Wielding Aefre, the blade singing in her hand, she slammed her shield into the face of one dark elf, stepped back and cut and slashed at two more. Soon, half the dark elves guarding the Vanir were dead or wounded and their companions were backing away. Svartálfar are courageous enough when led by a strong captain, but Kendra was in the other room and the chieftain of these particular elves had just been slain. Fear sprang into their faces and they started to retreat, clearly scared of the way in which Anna's sword flashed and flickered, dealing out death, the blade moving so fast it was just a blur of silver.

Wilburh helped them on their way. Stepping right out in front of them and swirling his arms around, he shouted a command: "*Gicelan dyngeas!*"

Out of the air above the heads of the dark elves, huge hailstones rained down on them – except that these were great lumps of ice, much larger than ordinary hailstones. They pulverised the Svartálfar, and after two of them were knocked senseless to the ground, the others did now turn and run, back past the figure of Raedann, apparently still alive, but bound in gold cord and fast asleep. On past the slumbering Vanir they ran, out through doors at the rear of the library and on deeper into the halls.

Wilburh slumped down onto his knees. "Quick, Anna, I'm exhausted," he gasped. "Release Ullr…"

She nodded. They could hear Kendra screeching at the guardian dwarves who were still battling with the dark elves in the throne room. Anna slipped off her cloak, unstrapped Gambantein and ripped off the cloth in which it was wrapped.

"Which one is Ullr?" she cried.

"That one over there." Wilburh pointed.

Holding the sword by the scabbard, Anna started forward. Kneeling down beside Ullr, she hesitantly laid the weapon on the floor and pulled off the scabbard. Finally, she removed the sheath from the hilt and tentatively wrapped her fingers around it to lift the sword from the floor. The moment she did so her eyes widened.

"Merciful Woden!" she gasped. "Gods of Æsir and Vanir protect me!" Then she let out a scream.

"What is it?" Wilburh asked. "What is happening?"

Anna did not answer. She was staring without seeing across the room and breathing rapidly. All the blood had drained from her face, leaving it a ghastly pale colour.

"Anna!" Lar shouted in alarm, running across the room and throwing himself down by her side. "Let go of the sword. Let me take it."

"No!" Slowly she shook her head then focused on Lar. "I can feel Gambantein and he is strong – so very strong," she whispered. "It is completely different to the Gjallarhorn. The horn was a companion, a friend. This…this is like…he

167

is drawing me in…as if he is the master and I the slave…I… I am losing myself…" She closed her eyes and swallowed hard.

"Anna! Please let go of the sword!" Lar shouted again, this time grasping her elbow and shaking her arm, but once more she refused. Then she opened her eyes, focusing again on her brother, her breathing more controlled.

"No…no, I will be fine, Lar. I just had to take control. It was as if we were having a conversation without words. I explained what we were doing and the sword's spirit has agreed to permit me to use the dark blade for this one task. Gambantein will obey me this once." She took a few deep breaths and then smiled a weak smile. "That was hard, but I am fine now, honestly."

Leaning over, Anna slipped the point of the blade under the golden cord wrapped around Ullr's sleeping body and sawed at his bonds. Gleipnir was of immense strength, beyond anything or anyone but a god to break, and yet beneath Gambantein's edge the threads parted like cotton to the blade of a knife.

They stared at Ullr. For a moment nothing happened, then his eyes twitched and he moved his head.

"He is coming round," Lar said with relief.

Wilburh smiled and, getting to his feet, ran over to the door then looked at the scene outside. The Dweorgar guardians were still heavily engaged in fighting the dark elves, while near the doorway, Hild was attempting to bind Gurthrunn's leg. Ellette stood over them with a loaded sling ever ready to cover them.

"The guardians seem to be winning," Wilburh reported over his shoulder to Anna and Lar. Then he whipped around to stare back into the throne room, because at that moment he heard a distant roar of rage. A roar he recognised.

"Merciful Woden!" Wilburh grimaced as he glanced towards the far doors. "So that's what Kendra was summoning with her flute!"

There, framed within the outer doorway, stood not one but three huge trolls. The beasts roared again as they broke into a run. The ground shook with every step they took as they thundered up the long hall, their huge stone clubs swinging wildly from side to side. A guardian took a blow squarely in his chest and was sent tumbling head over heels into one of the wooden thrones, which shattered as he crashed down upon it to lie motionless and bleeding. With grim faces, his Dweorgar companions turned to face the new danger.

To Wilburh's eyes, the guardians looked almost resigned to the near certain death that now threatened them, but he was not yet sufficiently recovered to conjure a strong enough spell to damage the giant trolls. He ran back to his companions. "Anna! Get cutting," he shouted. "Release the other gods!"

As the shield maiden hurried to do his bidding, Wilburh stared down at Ullr. Was the god trying to open his eyes? Yes, it seemed so. "Come on...come on, My Lord, please! Lord Ullr, please wake up or all is lost," he shouted.

Ullr's lips moved, then he lifted a hand for a moment before letting it drop again.

*Yes, the gods are waking, thought Wilburh, but how long will they take? They are needed now – right now!*

# CHAPTER TWENTY

## KENDRA'S PLAN

Leaving Ullr, Anna ran with Gambantein to Raedann and, bending over him, quickly cut his bonds. Not stopping to see if he began to stir, she headed on down the room, moving from god to goddess and goddess to god, slicing through their golden bonds as fast as she could. Even before she reached the last one, the first few Vanir were beginning to stir, yet it was taking time; much too much time. Glancing back at Raedann, she frowned with anxiety. Although his bonds had been severed before theirs, he appeared to be fast asleep still, a slight snore rumbling softly from his open mouth. *Suppose Gleipnir works differently with humans. Suppose the effect is greater than with gods and he never wakes up,* she thought. Biting her lip, Anna ran back to Ullr, looked down at the mighty sword in her hand, and whispering "Thank you" to the spirit blade, laid Gambantein on the ground beside Ullr's outstretched hand. He was not yet fully awake, but as Anna turned away she saw his eyelids flicker open and his fingers close around the hilt. There was nothing more that she could do for him.

Even above the noise of the battling dwarves, she could hear Kendra screaming with maniacal laughter each time one of the guardians was crushed. Grabbing up her shield, Anna sprinted to where Lar and Wilburh stood near the doorway, listening in horror to the guardians' cries and the roars of the advancing trolls.

"Come on, you two, hurry!" Anna gasped. "I have freed the gods. We can do no more in here and we are needed next door." Drawing Aefre from the scabbard at her waist, she plunged through the door, the boys at her heels.

Ellette and Hild were still standing over the crouching form of Gurthrunn. The dark elves, clearly encouraged by the trolls, were fighting with even more vigour than before, and Anna could see that Gurthrunn had been hit again, this time in the chest. Two javelins had pierced his chain shirt and stuck out at an angle. The armour had halted their momentum and the points had not gone as deep as they might have done, but even so, he was badly wounded and bleeding heavily. Ellette and Hild had apparently run out of sling stones, for they stood one on each side of the injured dwarf, each using her seax to keep the dark elves at bay, but it was clear that the two girls would shortly be overwhelmed.

Hefting her shield, Anna ran past them and threw herself back into battle against the nearest Svartálfar. Swinging her sword in a wide semi-circle, she drove the dark elves back, aware of Aefre singing in her grip as the blade sliced into the enemy.

Ahead the room was now swarming with dark elves. Maybe 100 of them were swirling around the four remaining guardians, but they seemed to be holding back a little, as though waiting for the trolls to do their work for them. These massive creatures stomped around, repeatedly bringing their huge clubs crashing down to swat at the dwarves. The trolls' movements were clumsy, but even so it took all of the Dweorgars' skill and prowess to avoid the mighty blows while at the same time dodging the dark elves' javelins. With axes and war hammers, they kept striking back, going for the trolls' legs and feet in an attempt to bring the giant creatures crashing to the floor, but succeeding only in slowing them down.

It was clear to Lar that the guardians would soon be crushed. With Anna now driving the Svartálfar back from Gurthrunn and the girls, he turned his attention to the battling dwarves. He had only a dozen arrows left and was determined to make each one count. Rapidly notching

arrows and letting fly, he hit dark elf after dark elf, even landed two on the trolls. The elves tumbled with each shot, but the trolls merely swatted the arrows away as if they were no more bothersome than flies.

Standing beside Lar, Wilburh, who after the few moments of respite in the library had regained a little of his strength, dredged deep for his power. As the pressure rose within him he began to pour fire and light, ice and stone into the dark elves. The first blast knocked twenty off their feet. He was not sure if he had killed or merely stunned them, but their comrades took one look at his raised hands and backed rapidly away.

Closing his ears to Kendra's cackling laughter, expecting that at any moment she would use her own powers against him, Wilburh turned his attention to one of the trolls, sending blast after blast of fire into its great body and driving the beast backwards. Finally, exhausted and almost drained of power, he sent a lightning bolt of intense crackling energy. With a great bang it hit the troll square in the face and the massive creature crashed to the ground, quite dead. Gasping for breath, Wilburh backed away, his legs trembling. Where was the Valkyrie and why was she not reacting? Perhaps she was simply enjoying watching the fighting, certain that her servants would win and not caring how many of them were killed or injured in the process. On his last legs, Wilburh summoned the dregs of his strength and, weakly drawing his seax, moved to cover Lar, who was now down to one arrow.

Still driving back the dark elves, Anna forced her way towards the two remaining trolls. Of the guardians, she now saw that only Hamaal was on his feet and still fighting, three of his companions dead, two severely wounded. She fought her way to his side and together they laid about the two trolls, but made little impact upon them. One caught Anna on the shoulder with its club and, crying out in pain, she dropped both her shield and sword and fell to the ground. The troll roared with laughter as it lifted the huge club ready to bring it down upon her defenceless body and pulverise her.

Yet, the blow never reached her.

Before the troll could finish its attack, it was hit by a massive bolt of fire. Killed instantly, it crumbled into a heap of charred stone. A moment later the other troll suffered the same fate.

Dazed with pain and struggling for breath, Anna turned her head and gasped in awe. Wilburh followed her gaze and felt his own jaw drop.

Standing in the doorway to the library was Ullr, Gambantein in his hand, flames lapping and licking along the edges of the great black blade as he pointed it at the remains of the trolls. It seemed as if the Vanir God had grown in stature since waking, for he almost filled the door frame. His eyes were fierce as he looked upon the scene of battle, and then he advanced into the fray. Emerging from the library at his back came his companions: a dozen Vanir gods.

They had been captured by Kendra, bound by Gleipnir, humiliated and eventually incapacitated. Now, freed from bondage, they were fully awake and very angry. They charged into battle against the Svartálfar; the full wrath of twelve vengeful gods and goddesses was directed against the remnants of the Valkyrie's dark elf army, and in a matter of moments, the battle was over.

Fifty dark elves were cut down. Others turned and ran screaming through the doors. Some of the gods headed off into the depths of the halls to seek out the elves that Anna and her companions had routed earlier, while others pursued the fleeing Svartálfar out of the doors and across the fields and woods of Vanaheim. The remaining gods, led by Ullr still wielding the flaming sword, turned and approached Kendra, who had returned to the throne and now sat there holding the mysterious clay pot on her lap.

Relief washed over Wilburh, making his legs tremble even more. Exhaustion seemed to seep into his bones and so he slumped down, content to watch the confrontation between the gods and the Valkyrie – yet looking at Kendra's face, Wilburh felt a curl of misgiving. *Why does she look so smug when all around her are defeated?*

"It is over, fallen one," boomed Ullr. "Your army is defeated and you, servant of Loki, are my captive. Give me that pot and surrender yourself. You will then be imprisoned until a court of the Æsir and the Vanir is assembled to judge you for your crimes, both here and elsewhere."

The gods and goddesses had also grown in size, and now they surrounded the Valkyrie, looming over her. Each one was armed, Ullr with one of the most powerful blades known in all the Nine Worlds, which made what happened next even more surprising to everyone except Wilburh.

Unarmed and alone, her army defeated, Kendra faced them – and laughed.

Grimly, Ullr reached out with one giant hand, obviously intending to seize the defiant Valkyrie. Yet, as he moved forward, his hand rebounded off an invisible barrier. He scowled at the sorceress then shook his head. "So you have erected an arcane barrier. That will delay us only moments, fallen one. Have you forgotten we are gods? It is we who invented the incantations you use. We can easily destroy this shield. Surrender, Kendra. You have lost."

Kendra laughed again. "You think you have won here this

day? Ask yourselves what you have achieved: a petty victory over lesser creatures such as dark elves and trolls? If you believe you have defeated *me* then you are as stupid as they. Everything that has happened has occurred exactly as I knew it would."

Gazing at her through the invisible barrier, Ullr frowned. "Do not try to deny the facts, Kendra. You have achieved nothing here save death and destruction, much of which we can repair."

The sorceress shrugged. "I will confess that I had hoped you Vanir would remain bound by Gleipnir for much longer. I wanted you removed from the struggle that is yet to come. And so you would have been had those interfering Midgard whelps not located the dark blade. But your imprisonment and the conquest of Vanaheim were not major parts of my plan, and it is of no significance to me that you are free."

While they were talking, Lar, still clutching his bow, had moved forward. "If that is so, why did you come to Vanaheim?" he asked, flexing the bowstring and notching his one remaining arrow.

Kendra turned her eyes on him. "Look at the pitiful boy with his toy bow and arrow!" she smirked. "The two items you retrieved for me – the pot and the cloak – they are what I came here for, Child of Midgard."

"Lucky for you we came here too then, otherwise you would never have been able to get your hands on them," Lar retorted. "The guardians would not have helped you. It is only by chance that we came along and you were able to make use of us. Suppose we hadn't?"

The Valkyrie laughed again. "Do you really believe it was chance, foolish boy?"

Lar frowned and glanced across at his friends. "I don't understand..."

"You came here seeking a magical means to defend your village. Why? Because of the attack from Niflheim. Who do you think suggested to the King of Niflheim that a raid on your village might be fruitful?"

"*You* did that?" Anna cried.

"Of course."

"Wait, though," said Hild, who in the momentary lull had removed the javelins from Gurthrunn's chest and was busy plugging his wounds with cloths to stem the bleeding. "We only came to Vanaheim because the Dweorgar here suggested it."

All heads turned to stare at her and Gurthrunn, who now raised himself painfully onto his elbow and said hoarsely, "Woden was keeping watch upon Scenestane. Each day he directed that one of his ravens fly over the village. When it returned with the report that you were under attack, I came at once. As I said, I had already intended going to Vanaheim because we had not heard from the Vanir in a few days and that seemed odd..." He trailed off and stared at Kendra. "You planned that also? You discovered I was already on the way to Vanaheim so you had the Niflheim attack Scenestane knowing I would go to its aid. You guessed that I, seeking to protect the village, would suggest the children came with me to speak to the Vanir. It was the obvious thing to do... but you knew that, didn't you."

Kendra nodded. "Bringing them right here where I needed them. I am grateful to you, Dweorgar," she sneered. "I knew you would not obey me unless I used them to force you. My only regret is that due to their ridiculous and somewhat unexpected heroics I did not manage to kill them on your return from the catacombs. Oh well," she laughed, "there is always the next time..."

"Next time?" Ullr snorted. "There will be no next time

for you, Kendra. You are our prisoner."

"No, Ullr, I am not," she said, shaking her head. "I won't be here for much longer…just long enough for two things. Firstly, for this!" With those words, she let the pot topple forward off her knees and fall to the ground where it shattered. The contents leaked out a dark viscous fluid that seeped through the reeds lining the floor and away. A sweet and at the same time alcoholic smell filled the air.

"The mead!" Ullr gasped in dismay.

Around him all the Vanir look horrified, several rushing forward and trying to salvage the liquid, but it was already too late.

"They seem awfully upset about a jar of mead," Lar observed to Wilburh. "I mean, if they get some honey they can make some more in a few weeks, can't they?"

Wilburh shook his head. "That is no ordinary mead, Lar."

"Really? What is it then?"

But Wilburh did not respond. He was watching Kendra. The Valkyrie was standing now, and he wondered why Ullr did not simply take her down. She was surrounded by Vanir gods who in a trice could shatter the barrier and grab hold of her. It was almost as if they did not believe it was really necessary. After all, what alternative did she have but to surrender? She was just salvaging her pride by delaying, but why were they letting her get away with it? Did they believe there was nothing she could do to them because they were gods? Wilburh, looking at her gleeful expression, was not so sure.

"That is my first aim achieved," she said, laughing at the gods' efforts to save the mead. "And now for the second!" With a flourish, she produced from behind her the cloak of falcon feathers and flung it across her shoulders.

"Take that off!" Ullr growled. At last he leapt towards Kendra, bursting through the barrier with one swipe of Gambantein, but he was too late, for where the Valkyrie had stood a magnificent falcon had appeared and was already soaring upwards, flapping its wings to gain the height of the rafters high above them.

The great bird hung in the air for a moment, and then, between one breath and the next, plummeted towards the ground, reached out with its claws and snatched Gambantein from Ullr's grasp. With a screech of triumph, the falcon shot out of the doors and away into the skies – and vanished.

It happened in the blink of an eye, and Ullr, roaring in frustration, was left grasping at the air through which the falcon had flown. Yet it was not the loss of the sword that appeared to bother him the most, for he switched his attention instantly to the ground and gazed at the shards of shattered pottery spread around his feet. Kneeling, he picked up a fragment and sniffed it.

Sitting back on his heels, he sighed heavily. "The Valkyrie has beaten us this day," he said to the Vanir. "Not as completely as she had hoped, but I fear this is a setback that will hurt us in the months to come."

The gods, who stood around staring down at the sodden reeds, nodded in agreement, their long faces registering their dismay.

Perplexed, Lar shook his head. "I don't understand, Lord Ullr. Why is the mead so important? Why are you all so downhearted by its loss? It's only a honeyed drink, after all."

Pushing himself onto his feet, Ullr moved across the room and threw himself heavily down on the throne Kendra had vacated. "Because not only is Kendra at large, but she has stolen Freya's cloak and destroyed the clay pot. It contained our supply of the magical mead that we Vanir gods use to see the future. It will take months to brew a new batch, and in the meantime we will not be able to see what evil Kendra is hatching in Svartálfaheimr while she rebuilds her army of dark elves."

"Ah...*that* is why it is so important," Lar said.

"Exactly so," Ullr said. "When we drink it we can direct our minds to see future events. We don't do it often as it diminishes our strength, which takes time to recover, but after Kendra opened the Bifrost, Woden asked us to use the mead to see what she was up to. Naturally we were concerned, but before we could retrieve the pot from the guardians, Kendra arrived in Vanaheim with Gleipnir and trapped us. She is cunning and powerful and we did not see it coming, fools that we are."

He fell silent, and into the silence, Wilburh spoke. "You realise what this means?" They all looked at him. "None of what has happened was an accident," he explained. "Kendra *is* planning something – she near enough said so when she spoke of the struggle yet to come. Whatever it is, she wants the gods blind to it. That is why she broke the pot."

Ullr nodded. "It is even worse now that she has Freya's cloak. As you saw, she can transform into a falcon, which is more important than you might imagine. That cloak allows its wearer to fly not only through the skies, but also between the Nine Worlds. She does not even need the Bifrost. She is free to go wherever she likes and there is no way to track her or tell where she might be heading. We believe that she plans one day to free Loki, but we do not know how. The stolen cloak and the wasted mead must have something to do with it. Yet the gods are blind and she can go where she will." Ullr sighed. "Just what is she up to?"

"Don't forget," said Wilburh, who had just had a thought, "that she also took Gambantein from you. Maybe she plans to use it to free Loki from his bonds."

"Perhaps so." Ullr nodded.

Anna disagreed. "Possibly, but I don't think Gambantein could have been part of her plan. She seemed genuinely surprised when she discovered we had it. I think she grabbed the sword on the spur of the moment – it was a definite bonus for her. She may one day use it to try to free Loki, but I don't think that is her plan – at least not yet. I think she has something else in her mind to do first. The problem is, none of us has a clue what." Anna paused, frowning in

181

thought. "It is strange that she seemed not to care when we managed to free you, for that definitely wasn't part of the plan. She must have been supremely confident that she could outwit you."

Ullr grimaced. "Yes, and it is I who is at fault. I was gulled by false pride, thinking there was nothing she could do against us gods once we were free. In the heat of the moment I had forgotten about Freya's cloak." He banged his clenched fist on the arm of the throne, the sound reverberating in the hall. "Woden's teeth! I should have forestalled her while I had the chance."

There was silence for a while, then he turned to the children. "We owe you for our freedom, for without your courage we would yet be imprisoned in that golden thread. As I understand it, you came here looking for our aid in protecting your village in Midgard. How ironic then that it was we who were protected by you! We will provide you an enchantment to protect Scenestane while the Bifrost remains open. Know this: henceforth the Vanir and your people are friends. To defeat Kendra we will need to trust each other and act together. I do not need the mead to tell me that a difficult time lies ahead for us all. Mischief throughout the Nine Worlds is surely the Valkyrie's master plan. It pleases me that the Æsir and the Vanir stand together with the people of Midgard and our Dweorgar friends against whatever Loki and Kendra have in mind. The battle you have just endured has not been without cost: it grieves me that you have lost three of your companions, Hamaal. I can only hope their sacrifice is not in vain."

Hamaal bowed. "They will be honoured to have fought for the Vanir, Lord Ullr. Never fear, by now they will be feasting in Valhalla, and when our wounds are healed we three will return to the catacombs. We will recruit other Dweorgar to join us and will once more guard your treasures."

At this moment, stretching and yawning, Raedann emerged from the library. "Did someone say treasures? What treasures are those? Where? I don't see any tr..." Eyes popping, his voice trailed away as he looked around at the room strewn with bodies and the charred remains of the trolls, then at the wounded Gurthrunn and finally at the children.

"I seem to have been asleep. Did I miss anything?"

For the first time in days, the children burst out laughing.

# Chapter Twenty-One

## Home Again

Two days later the companions prepared to set off back through the Bifrost to Midgard. It had taken that long for Gurthrunn, who had lost a lot of blood, to gain enough strength to travel. Hild had kept close to the Goddess Nerthus, who had healed the injured dwarves' hurts using potions that were new to Wilburh's twin. She eagerly learnt as much as she could about them, and, directed by Nerthus, had been out collecting unfamiliar plants and herbs. Ellette had kept her company, hunting for sling stones to replenish their supply. Lar and Anna, eager to show Raedann the treasures, had persuaded Hamaal to take them back to the catacombs. Of them all, only Wilburh had stayed indoors, using the time to study in the library and to learn more of the arcane arts. Ullr, true to his word, had supplied him with a scroll of rune paper containing the script he would need to protect Scenestane.

Just before they departed, the god also gave the boy a large bound book. "Herein lies an encyclopaedic knowledge of the mystical arts. Study it well, Sorcerer of Midgard, and you will grow into a powerful man – maybe even as powerful as Merlin himself. I am impressed by your skills, Wilburh, but use them wisely. Use them only for good and to protect your people."

Wilburh bowed. "Divine Ullr, I thank you. I have learnt much this last week, and most important of all is precisely that lesson. My power exists to protect those I care about, and that is exactly how I will use it."

Then they left, walking back to the entwined trees that

formed the Vanaheim portal into the Bifrost. Gurthrunn went to touch the runes that would take them to Midgard, but Wilburh moved to stand in front of him. "No need for that," he said. "Follow me." Without waiting for a reply, he stepped across the threshold.

The last time he had journeyed through the Bifrost, Wilburh had felt that he should be able to control it, if he only knew how. This time he did know how, and without even thinking about it he commanded the rainbow bridge to take him where he and his companions wished to go. Awestruck by his growing powers, they followed at his heels.

A few moments later the Sorcerer of Midgard was standing on the grass next to the barrow, just north of Scenestane.

"Wilburh?" a familiar voice asked. It was Juliana. She was in front of him, a basket in one hand and shears in the other. Meccus and Nerian were close by, fully armoured and armed with spears, while another half dozen villagers also stood on guard.

"Mother, what are you doing here?" Wilburh asked her.

For a moment it looked as if she was about to rush forward and fling her arms around him, but perhaps mindful of embarrassing him she simply smiled. "Well, right now I am collecting marigold flowers – there is a crop growing on the barrow."

"No, I mean what are you all doing right here?"

Juliana glanced around at Meccus and Nerian. "Truth be told, we have kept a watch most of the last few days. We are your parents – you and the others are young. We were just worried. Proud of you, but worried." She bit her lip, her face a little strained. "Is your sister with you? Is she safe?"

"Both," he said shortly, preoccupied. "You're proud? Even of me and my strange interests in magic and sorcery?"

His mother looked embarrassed. "Yes, son, proud both of you and of that, though I don't understand it at all. I know I said some silly things, but I have come to realise that your talents are important to the village and that makes me proud," she said, this time ignoring his pink cheeks and hugging him anyway. At this moment Hild emerged from the Bifrost, followed by Anna, Lar, Ellette and finally Raedann and Gurthrunn.

"That was remarkable, boy," called the Dweorgar. "You just commanded the Bifrost and it obeyed you!"

"Show off," teased Lar, "and after all that stuff you just said to Ullr about only using your powers to protect us." He grinned.

"Even so, it was awesome," chipped in Anna, coming with Hild and Ellette to stand beside her brother.

Wilburh smiled at them. "Yes, well I picked up a few skills in Vanaheim, and that one was fun, true. Yet I did not do it to show off. It was necessary for what Ullr and I have planned for me to do to protect Scenestane. You will see."

Lar quirked an eyebrow. "So, go on, tell us…" but by then Nerian and Meccus had rushed over to them and the moment was lost.

Meccus embraced Ellette, and Juliana now moved to Hild and hugged her, while Nerian reached Lar and Anna. Lar stepped aside to allow their father to embrace Anna, but was surprised when Nerian pulled him into his arms first.

"What?" Lar said, bemused.

"I was wrong not to show you the same affection as Anna in front of the villagers, son. Meccus told me you were upset and I am sorry. I love you both equally, of course I do."

His ears pink, Lar returned the embrace and smiled at his father. "I had wondered," he murmured. "I love you too, Pa."

187

"So then," Nerian said gruffly, turning to Wilburh and Gurthrunn, "did you manage it?"

Wilburh nodded.

"So, a successful mission then," Nerian said. "Any complications?" He eyed the bandages around the dwarf's chest. "I see you are wounded, Gurthrunn."

"Just a scratch, Nerian. There were one or two complications, we will tell you about them later."

"Oh? You do have the spell to protect us though?" Nerian frowned at Wilburh.

Again Wilburh nodded. Tucking the precious book under one arm, he produced a roll of parchment from beneath his tunic. "Everything we need is written in this scroll," he said. "I can show you now, if you like."

Nerian grunted. "Go ahead."

Unrolling the scroll, Wilburh turned and recited the words on the rune paper. A glittering dome, so clear it was almost transparent, sprang up – not over the villagers, but centred on the barrow and encompassing the Bifrost.

Nerian stared at it in awe, then put out a hand. Grunting with effort, he pressed against the dome. "How can such a flimsy looking thing be so hard and unyielding?" he asked.

"Magic. It is an arcane shield," Gurthrunn explained.

"Similar to the one I created in the throne room during the battle," Wilburh said as an aside to the others.

Juliana instantly pricked up her ears. "Battle? What bat…"

"Later, Mother," Wilburh said, cutting her off in mid-flow.

"But Kendra destroyed that shield, strong as it was," Anna pointed out.

"Yes, she did. But I had flung it up in desperation and with no preparation, relying on my own power. Kendra is at least as strong as I. She was able to shatter it with ease. This shield, however, takes power direct from the Bifrost itself, and that power is limitless. The shield will withstand 1,000 lightning bolts. Any creature that cares to come against us, including ice elementals, will not get through it, and yet a friend may pass through it at will – that is, providing I permit it, for it will answer only to me."

"So that is why you did your little trick with the Bifrost?" Lar asked, impressed.

"Yes, I needed to link to the Bifrost, to feel its power and learn to command it. Ullr told me how. He said that once I'd done that, I would be able to use it to power the shield. And so I have."

"So we are safe again?" Nerian asked.

"Safe for now, certainly, yet..." Wilburh hesitated "...I think we need to tell you what happened in Vanaheim, Nerian," he said, exchanging a grim glance with Anna.

"Good idea." The Headsman nodded. "But before you do we will return to the village and I will send for Iden. He will want to know how you got on, Wilburh." Glancing once more at the glistening shield, Nerian turned to lead the way. "Come," he roared, "back to the hall, everyone, let us open some mead."

"How very appropriate to the tale," Raedann murmured with a wink at Lar, the two of them joining the throng as the villagers, shouting their approval, all fell in behind Nerian and headed down the path.

Or almost everyone, for after they had gone a solitary figure stood on the barrow, studying his handiwork with satisfaction, his gaze on the shimmering dome. Relief flooded through him. Believing he was alone, Wilburh thrust his fist into the air and shouted, "YES! I *did* it!"

Becoming aware of a movement in the nearby trees, he

swung round and saw his mother emerge, clutching her basket of marigolds. Calling out to him, she beckoned.

"Come on, son, hurry along. Whatever it is you did, it is time to go home now."

He grinned. "Coming, Mother," then Wilburh, Sorcerer of Midgard, turned away from the Bifrost and went home.

## THE END

# About Vanaheim

In Anglo-Saxon and Norse mythology, Vanaheim is mentioned as one of the Nine Worlds. However, not as much is known about it as other worlds, such as Asgard. What then can we say about it? What did the Anglo-Saxons believe about this world and its inhabitants?

Vanaheim was the home world of the Vanir gods. These gods were considered a distinctly different race to the Æsir gods of Asgard. They were often associated with having power over the weather, fertility, and crops and the harvest. Their world is described as having gentle winds and refreshing rain. The Vanir were also thought to have more wisdom than the Æsir, and possibly to have discovered the powers of magic before the Æsir did. They were also supposed to have had the ability to see into the future.

# The Æsir-Vanir War

Not all the Vanir were good natured. One of them was a witch called Gullweig who travelled to Asgard to try to get gold from the Æsir by trickery. When the Æsir discovered her they killed her. The Vanir did not like this and a great war occurred – the first war in prehistory. Both sides were gods and so were powerful, and the war raged on without conclusion. Eventually the Vanir actually breached the defences of Asgard, but could not defeat Woden's forces. The stories tell of great damage and harm to both Asgard's and Vanaheim's armies. In the end, however, peace was made. To guarantee the peace, hostages were exchanged. Two Asgardians went to Vanaheim while three Vanir gods went to Asgard.

191

# WHO WERE THE VANIR?

We do not know as many names of the Vanir as we do of the Æsir. Most of the stories and legends are of the Æsir gods. But we do know a few. Firstly these included the three gods who went to Asgard at the end of the war – the God Njord and his son Frey and daughter Freya.

*Njord* was the god of winds at sea and would fill the sails of ships. He would also blow out wild fires in forests if he saw them.

*Freya* was the same Goddess Freya who was mentioned in *Shield Maiden*, and who possessed the Brisingamen and the Falcon Cloak. Her brother *Frey* was a god of fertility, which means that he helped plants and animals to grow and have young. His symbol was a boar after his own magical boar on which he rode through the heavens in midsummer, encouraging the sun to shine longer, and he helped the crops to grow by mixing sunlight and rain. When the Anglo-Saxons held feasts and ceremonies in his honour they would cook boar. Frey owned a sword called Gambantein. (See About Gambantein below.)

These three had left Vanaheim and lived in Asgard. Do we know any names of the other Vanir? Kvasir was a Vanir God known for his great wisdom, but he was killed. (See *About the Mead* below).

*Ullr* appears to have been a Vanir God and a warrior god, perhaps also a god of hunting. In fact he was worshipped quite early in our history, possibly dating back to prehistory. There are early references to him in inscriptions and jewellery. He is depicted as having a bow and arrow. He also is often shown as wearing skis – presumably to travel round the snow-covered Scandinavian landscape. He is still a patron saint of winter sports in Northern Europe. He only appears in the earliest Norse sagas and vanishes from the later stories.

We also know of *Nerthus*: a Vanir goddess associated with fertility. She is mentioned by the Roman historian Tacitus in his First Century account of the Germanic peoples. Tacitus tells us that Nerthus represented Mother Earth and brought peace and plenty. He describes how once a year the high priest would drive an enclosed golden chariot around Nerthus's holy island. The goddess herself was thought to be inside. Wherever she passed men would lay down their weapons and tools, and under her blessing war and work would cease for a while.

So Nerthus and Ullr were more ancient gods. This fact, and the fact that the entire Vanir race was mostly ignored by the later sagas, might mean that the Vanir were worshipped by one group of Germanic-Scandinavian tribes and the Æsir by another. The latter group were perhaps more powerful, and although the myths include them both, more attention is given to the Æsir.

# About the Mead

As has already been mentioned, the Vanir were able to see the future. This was actually accomplished by making a special form of mead. Mead is similar to beer or cider, but is made from honey and is a sweet-smelling and tasting alcohol. Often made by monks and drunk almost exclusively in Wales, in Anglo-Saxon times, mead, like beer, would have been drunk by children as well as adults, but batches produced for common drinking were much less alcoholic. The story goes that the Vanir had a special recipe that gave them the power of foretelling. This was made from honey, but also the blood of a wise Vanir god called Kvasir, who was killed by evil dwarves – or possibly dark elves. The mead is mentioned a number of times in the Norse legends, and often is referred to as the 'Mead of Poetry'.

# About Gambantein

Gambantein was a powerful sword. The gods possessed a number of powerful swords, and Gambantein belonged to the Vanir God, Frey. It was said to be able to float and fight by itself, and so was presumably intelligent. It could shine like the sun and maybe burst into flames. Magical runes added to it enabled it to suck life out of a foe or age them. The legends do indeed say that Frey gave it away to his servant as a reward for the servant arranging a marriage between him and Gerdr, the giantess. The servant actually threatened Gerdr with the sword to get her to agree! When she first met Frey she fell in love with him anyway, so perhaps Frey would have been better just talking to her in the first place!

# The Falcon Cloak

Freya owned a suit or cloak made of Falcon feathers which was capable of transforming the wearer into a falcon. She could use it to fly around the Nine Worlds.

If you are interested in knowing more about the Norse gods, you will find additional information, along with the runic alphabet used by Wilburh, at the back of *Shield Maiden*, the first book in this series.

## Wilburh's Spells

Much of this book is about Wilburh and his struggle to gain mastery over magic: a mastery that he will need in the fight against Kendra and Loki. Here are the spells he uses in this book. They use Old English words – the language the Anglo-Saxons spoke from around AD 400 till after the Norman Conquest in 1066.

*Heoruflá æledfýr:* fire + arrow – a bolt of fire.

*Lyffc bordrand:* air + shield – a defensive dome.

*Sunne Ablaedan:* sun + blind – a blinding spell.

*Egorstréamas:* water stream – a blast of water.

*Windræs:* storm of wind – a blast of air.

*Abéonne rápas:* command + rope – rope control spell.

*Ádæle:* apart or away – separation spell.

*Æledfýr blæstas:* fire + blast – a cone of fire.

*Gicelan dyngeas:* ice + storm – summoning hailstones.

ALSO BY RICHARD DENNING

# HOURGLASS INSTITUTE SERIES

## Tomorrow's Guardian

ISBN 978-0-9564835-6-0

*Time travel sounds like fun until you try it!*

Tom Oakley experiences disturbing episodes of déjà-vu and believes he is going mad. Then, he discovers that he's a 'Walker' – someone who can transport himself to other times and places.

Tom dreams about other 'Walkers' in moments of mortal danger: Edward Dyson killed in a battle in 1879; Mary Brown who perished in the Great Fire of London; and Charlie Hawker, a sailor who drowned on a U-boat in 1943. Agreeing to travel back in time and rescue them, Tom has three dangerous adventures before returning to the present day.

But Tom's troubles have only just begun. He finds that he's drawn the attention of evil individuals who seek to bend history to their will. Soon, Tom's family are obliterated from existence and Tom must make a choice between saving them and saving his entire world.

# The Praesidium Series

## The Last Seal
ISBN: 9780956810397

*Gunpowder and sorcery in 1666...*

Seventeenth century London – two rival secret societies are caught in a battle that threatens to destroy the city and beyond. When a truant schoolboy, Ben, finds a scroll revealing the location of magical seals that bind a powerful demon beneath the city, he is thrown into the centre of a dangerous plot that leads to the Great Fire of 1666.

*An awesome array of characters which definitely included the good, the bad and the ugly, and an amazing plot!*
*This young adult historical fantasy had me totally engrossed, and I would recommend it to anyway who loves historical fantasy/fiction (especially British) whether you're a teen or an adult.*

The Slowest Bookworm

*Denning has a real thirst for historical knowledge and this certainly shines through in his books, with his descriptions of London in 1666 making you feel as if you were in the middle of the raging fire.*

YA Yeah Yeah
Winner of a B.R.A.G. Medallion

Lightning Source UK Ltd.
Milton Keynes UK
UKOW06f0219060615

253002UK00001B/20/P